EACH LIFE IS A NOVEL

a novel

Dilek Ozsoyler

Kindle Direct Publishing

kindle direct publishing

To My Dear Husband and Sons...
I owe a lot to my dear husband İbrahim, my dear sons Ege and Güney, whose support I always felt while writing my novel during these pandemic days. They supported me a lot while writing my novel and I love them very much.

I wrote this novel during the covid-19 pandemic, which was intense, took a lot away from people's souls and caused people to question themselves. Writing is a pleasure for me. I hope you enjoy reading my novel.

CONTENTS

EACH LIFE IS A NOVEL (A NOVEL)

PERSONALITIES DEVELOPED WITH TRAUMA

**SOMETIMES YOU CAN NOT RESIST
THE IMPOSITIONS OF LIFE...**

1) THE JOURNEY OF EMİN AND GÜL... 1980

When Emin opened his eyes in the morning, the sun brightened up his day as it filled the room. He got up from the bed in one fell swoop. Emin, a blue-eyed, handsome, and burly man of forty years old, stretched and went to the bathroom. There he did his business, shaved and whistled, and headed for the kitchen. He inhaled the scent of coffee that spread to the whole house.

"Hımm… The best smell in the world!" he said as he entered the kitchen.

"Good morning guys," he called out and kissed his daughter Zeynep on the cheek. She looked at him with furrowed eyebrows. Realizing that something was wrong, Emin stroked the head of his son Cem and poured himself a cup of coffee. Returning to his wife Füsun,

"What's the matter?" he asked looking at her curiously. She continued to grumble without paying attention to him:

"I'm tired of your mess," she said. Cem said,

"Zeynep forgot her book at school, so she couldn't do her

homework, that's why mom is angry." Füsun, on the other hand, continued to grumble,

"I don't know when you're going to get smarter?" she said. As Zeynep kept yelling,

"I gave it to Eda, I forgot it because she didn't give it back to me!". Emin knew better than to get involved in these dialogues between his children and his wife. Whenever he did, the issue got bigger and wandered away from the subject. Emin mostly took his children's side, trying to defend them, which infuriated Füsun. Similar things happened so many times. Their discussions on this subject mostly ended with Füsun accusing him of being unconcerned by their children's problems and acting irresponsibly. So he preferred to remain silent now for his own comfort.

His wife was usually very agitated in the mornings; she would give orders to the children around and get furious if something went wrong.

Emin did not like such morning routines. So many times he thought to himself, 'I wish we had better mornings.'

Emin was an assistant physician at the internal medicine department when his affair with his wife Füsun, who was also a doctor, began. He was the son of a rich landlord who owned a large farm and citrus orchards in Adana, the heart of Çukurova. The whole family was very happy when he got into Adana Anatolian High School. He was the only member who got higher education in the family, and everyone was proud of him. On top of that, when he got into the medical faculty in Ankara, his family used every financial and moral means available, and they were ready to do whatever he asked. He had a very colorful student life with a lot of money. Emin had a colorful personality, he immediately found a place for himself in any community he joined and he always had a positive outlook on life.

Until a few weeks ago, Emin had to force himself to get out of bed in the mornings, the thought of going to Mersin from Adana for work filled him with weariness, and he would almost crawl to the bathroom. The struggle for life that started with the sunrise continued all day long and ended with going to bed at night was now boring him. Waking up early, having a very long way to go, exhausting work conditions, shifts, bureaucracy to deal with, the hospital administration, and the patients with their never-ending demands were distressing him all day long. He also had a few annoying lawsuits filed by patients that kept his mind busy all the time. These lawsuits were pouring fuel on the fire. He had been tired and unhappy for a long time, both physically and mentally.

Since the birth of his son Yiğit, who was now three years old, he and Füsun, unfortunately, became distant with each other, and tension became the prevailing feeling in their affair. Füsun, who had to deal with the problems of the three children, was overwhelmed by her routines at work and at home, and this reflected on the family as constant irritability and intolerance. Emin, who was already returning home from work very reluctantly, was barely helping her.

Sometimes he became aware of his children's problems after a long while when it was too late to find a solution. On weekdays, he would have a little conversation with the children, stroke their hair, have a forced couple of words with his wife, and go to work. By the time he got home at nine in the evening, his children would already be asleep or they would be about to go to bed. Especially after the birth of their third child, Füsun's priorities changed; lately, Emin was barely able to find a place for himself among her priorities.

But such mornings have not been affecting him much anymore for a month now, because he has been very happy.

He knew the reason for the heart thumps he felt, the sunny days he was more aware of, and the desire to work out more, but he was afraid to admit it even to himself. The reason for these feelings was a woman. A woman who meant nothing to him before, but as he got to know her, he felt how meaningless it was to live without her.

In a little while, he would pick her up from her house and they would go to work together. Despite living in Adana, Dr. Emin had been commuting to Mersin for two years. He has been working there as an internist at a private hospital.

It was Dr. Gül, who worked at the same health center as Füsun, who made Emin experience the feelings that he thought were a thing of the past, who made his heart rate accelerate and his hands and feet twitch.

Although she lived in Adana with her family as well, she was assigned to Mersin by the directorate due to a need for a doctor, which was planned to last for three months. At first, Gül wasn't happy with this situation. But then somehow, she thought three months would pass in the blink of an eye, and she accepted her fate. Moreover, this assignment could be good for her since she had problems with her husband. Small one-hour trips in the morning and evening could be an opportunity for her to be alone with herself and to think about things about her private life.

It was Füsun who made an offer to Gül, saying, "Emin goes there by car every day anyway, you should go with him."

"I don't know, I don't want to bother Mr. Emin," Gül objected at first.

"No way, why should you bother him? Emin told me that he was feeling sleepy a few times before he left in the morning. You can make him talk and keep him from getting sleepy, it'll put my mind at ease too," Füsun replied.

"Also, you wouldn't be bored by going that road alone. And you won't get tired by driving more than two hours a day," she said as if giving advice. She had made this offer to Gül during a dinner with her colleagues from the health center. Emin was there too, and he didn't like that Füsun made such a fait accompli without asking him.

"How could you do something like that without asking me? Do I want to travel for hours with someone I don't know?" he said furiously when they returned home that day in the evening.

"Why, don't you know Gül? We came together with them in dozens of meetings," said Füsun.

"How many hours in total have I talked to her?" Emin asked gruntingly.

"Trust me, you will like Gül. She always has positive energy," said Füsun.

In fact, it was Füsun who paved the way for the blow to her life and the betrayal against her. If she had guessed that something bad was going to happen, she probably wouldn't have even mentioned this well-intentioned offer. If she had known that Gül's temporary assignment would even be extended a few more times, she wouldn't have winked and jokingly added,

"We wouldn't mind if you split the gas money either!".

There was a formality and distance in the first days of Emin and Gül's commute to Mersin and back. Emin's anger towards Füsun, who got him involved in this situation, did not go away for a long time, and at first, he did not speak unless he had to, he did not feel like talking at all. In rare conversations, they were talking about professional matters, and sometimes about the weather. How long did they share the car like two strangers, side by side, neither of them could remember. But over time, they inevitably started to have ideas about each other.

For example, Emin felt that he was starting to like Gül's style and demeanor, and he started to think that she was a 'very intelligent woman' by the way she talked. Gül, on the other hand, started to think that driving suited him very well and that he was a 'very sexy man.' Gül also realized how peaceful and happy she was as she sat in the passenger's seat.

After commuting like this for a week or two, they got into the car one evening after work, exhausted. Gül noticed that Emin was extremely angry. Emin, who did not speak at all on the way, seemed to take his anger out on the gear shift and the steering wheel, and these movements betrayed his mood even though he was not aware of it. With his brows furrowed, thoughts in his head, he acted as if Gül wasn't there as he drove in silence.

"You don't need to pick me up starting from tomorrow," said Gül, breaking the silence. Emin, who came to his senses with Gül's voice, said,

"Sorry?" as he snapped out of his thoughts. She decided that it would be appropriate to say that she would no longer be traveling with him, as she felt that Emin was uncomfortable with her in the car and had long felt uneasy about her own feelings. Although she did not intend to get a doctor's report,

she lied saying, "I got time off from work to be with my daughters, I may extend it with a doctor's report at the end, I don't know yet." When her time off was over, she would no longer get in that car to go to Mersin.

"I'm sorry, I had a bad day," Emin apologized. "Okay," Gül simply said, nodding slowly.

Emin understood the value of his travels with Gül when she was not there. In her absence, he understood how nice it was to have Gül in the car, how calming her voice was, and how her optimistic attitude was good for him. Without her, the road never seemed to end.

When the first week was about to end, he plucked up all his

courage and called her house.

"I was wondering how many days of absence you'll get," he was saying on the phone. Gül was surprised by this call. Gathering all his courage, he added, "I have got used to traveling with you, it will make me happy to take you from your home again." He would later confess to Gül how difficult it was to utter these sentences.

After ten days, they began to travel together again. During the time they were apart, they had realized that breathing the same air made both of them happy.

The pressure of being married to other people and having children prevented them from acting more naturally, and neither of them dared to reveal their feelings. As soon as they realized that they were attracted to each other, they started to get closer. Their conversations started to be more sincere and filled with jokes.

Over time, the topics of these conversations also changed and became more private. Gül was touching upon the most sensitive points and making him open up to her. Emin, on the other hand, was discovering new things about himself during these conversations and he did not know how he could tell Gül the things about himself that he would not share with anyone else. But every time he poured out his heart, he felt relieved as if he had confessed.

Gül was a good listener and a good confidant. The more she listened, the more she got to know Emin and began to like this man who made her laugh with his funny jokes. She felt that she had nothing to hide from him. She was sharing everything with this man and releasing the shreds of conscience that had bothered her so much at the beginning.

When he shared something with his wife, her remarks were usually judgmental and discouraging. Gül, on the other hand, would silently listen to what he told, then she would offer a different perspective, surprising Emin and impressing him with her different attitude. Emin enjoyed her encouraging words when he was indecisive about something, her seeing the ironic side of events and making jokes about people, and he admired her childlike excitement and how she surrendered her spirit to him.

There was more than just conversations: the chemistry between them when Gül's fingers touched Emin's as she handed him the sandwiches she prepared at home some mornings, his heartbeat getting faster when their eyes met, and their hands staying together for a long time to say goodbye when she was leaving.

Emin knew that it was a bad idea to have an affair with a married woman. Especially if this woman is your wife's friend if your children are friends if her husband is a lawyer, and if you are a well-known doctor in Adana. Emin knew all this, but he believed that greater powers were at play in this extraordinary event. He used to keep on saying to himself that everything was possible in life, and he seemed not worried about the flow of life. Although her family life was not very bright either, he realized with sadness that she had not even had a chance to question it and consider what she could do about it until now.

Gül was an intellectual; she was a calm, confident person. She would listen to those in need and would come to the aid of those in distress. She was the elder child of lawyer parents with two daughters. She had a sister named Lale. She had graduated from Ege University Faculty of Medicine in Izmir, the city where she lived with her family. She chose clothes that suited her plump body from authentic clothing stores, and she liked to wear large and colorful jewelry that suited her. Her hair had been short for as long as she could remember, and it suited her little face very well. She had been planning to end her marriage that was not going well for a long time and she had been waiting for the right time to tell this to her husband.

One weekend morning in Adana, Emin was taking his son Cem to a class as the bright blue sky dazzled the eyes, and Barış Manço's song was playing on the radio as Emin sang the lyrics loudly:

The weather is frosty, my hands are in my pockets
I sing a song, can you hear it?
I don't have a door to knock on; I long for happiness,
The streets are mine now, do you see it?

Surprised that Emin was shaking his head to the upbeat song and not being accustomed to seeing him like this, Cem said, "What's up dad, you're so cheerful today!". He laughed out loud and replied,

"Yes sonny, I love this song very much!". He felt young and happy at that time. He was working happily all day during the week – he was no longer angry at the hospital administration and bureaucracy as he used to be - every day as the evening approached to travel back, he felt excited like high school students. He believed that this beautiful feeling of love that surrounded him with confidence would go on and on.

As time went by and their relationship progressed, the number of days when they stopped on the way and had a coffee or tea during the travels between Mersin and Adana started to increase. Those stops evolved into dinners. They were entering small towns and villages on the road and exploring those places. Not knowing the region well, Gül saw lots of new places. Tarsus, Yenice, Pozantı, Gülek... Located in Taş Altı on Gülek Plateau over the Taurus Mountains, "Mümin's Place," where they stopped frequently when they got hungry, welcomed them with its nature, greenery, bird calls, and delicious meat chops. There were many times when they enjoyed pastry cheese rolls called "sıkma" and yogurt drinks called *"ayran."* Being together at the magnificent Tarsus Waterfall formed by the Berdan River and breathing the fresh air together was priceless.

Emin's voice speaking of historical places filled with nature's wonder around them sounded as smooth as velvet to Gül's ears while she was gazing far away as his hands moved gently on Gül's silky hands. Their touches on each other were enough to excite them like they were in a world of dreams.

The tone of Gul's voice, her little stresses when talking, and her occasional laughter reawakened all the nice feelings inside Emin, compelled him to look at her with compassion, and prevented him from looking at somewhere else but her. Despite Emin's insistency, Gül repeatedly refused to have an affair with him by saying that she would not cheat on her husband as a married woman.

She learned all the things she knew then from Emin, such as that the place passing by Gulek Strait, the gateway connecting the Mediterranean to Central Anatolia Region, was called 'Cilician Gate'; that the gate where the famous queen of Egypt, Cleopatra, and her lover Roman General Antonius entered the city to meet in Tarsus was called Cleopatra's Gate for that reason; the legend telling that a king, who learned from a fortuneteller that her daughter would be bitten by a snake and die, ordered the construction of Maiden's Castle, historically known as Korykos, for the safety of his daughter but a snake entering into a basket of grapes bit the princess and killed her; that the minstrel Karacaoglan was also born on the Taurus Mountains. They were now familiar with the factories, perfectly plowed fields, citrus gardens, and cotton fields they saw along the road.

Gül submitted a petition to the Health Directorate stating that she was willing to go to Mersin and extend her temporary duty for another three months. In this way, commuting between Adana and Mersin for three more months made them feel like young lovers with their feet swept off the ground, rather than people who are married with children, and they couldn't wait to see each other.

Towards the end of the sixth month, they began to question their relationship and talk about what to do. They felt helpless in the face of this sudden, unpredictable relationship. They had to do something, yes, but what?

Either they would face their families and confess everything by taking the risk, or they would give up on this love and go their own way. After a long time of thinking and many sleepless nights, they decided on the first option, but then they couldn't dare to do it. It was not easy to risk what would happen after explaining everything to their families. It wasn't easy to tear apart their families to be together, of course, but the thought of not being together was also very painful. When their conscience did not leave them alone, Gül did not extend her temporary appointment even when she had the chance to do so, which she happily did before, and returned to her workplace in Adana.

They continued their daily lives separately for a month or two, but they soon realized that they could not continue like this. Because Gül had begun to feel like a lost soul. Nothing gave her joy anymore. She could not concentrate on the book she was reading, and she was walking away when someone was talking to her about something.

How many times has her daughter Alya reproached her saying, "You are not listening to me, mom." She was always confused. In the health center, however, she could not look into Füsun's eyes, she was leaving the room the moment Füsun entered.

Although she replied, "No, there is absolutely nothing," Füsun asked.

AN AUTHORITARIAN FATHER CAN MAKE YOU A STRICT PERSON IN THE FUTURE

2) FÜSUN'S YOUTH AND MARRIAGE TO EMİN... 1966

Füsun was born and raised in Adana, and she believed that life should be taken seriously. She was hesitant to show her emotions, but she would get her claws out the moment someone stepped on her toes. The social values were important to her, and she did not see any harm in living her life according to these values. Her father was a police officer who had served in various parts of the country and settled in Adana when he retired; her mother was a housewife who was extremely fond of her home and children. Füsun, as the daughter of a police officer, had to leave many of her friends behind because they moved a lot, so she strongly felt that she did not belong to any city, and her student life at the medical school was uneventful. Two or three friends, with whom she was very close, constituted her social circle, she did have other friends and did not participate in social activities. Theater, cinema, picnics, teas, parties were not for her. Her father would not have taken kindly to her being involved in such activities anyway. Mr. Mustafa, who raised his children traditionally, according to the customs of the society, was proud of raising a doctor devoted to her country and nation. The way his parents raised him and the way he raised his children had not changed much over the years. Whatever he learned from his father was right in his eyes. He thought showing love to children is a weakness, and he would always assert his authority at home through his behavior.

He could easily take his anger out on Mrs. Meryem if something went wrong without even asking her anything, and he did not hesitate to commit all kinds of physical and psychological violence. Mr. Mustafa was a father who thought that control should not be given up until he found honest husbands for his daughters. He wanted a son so much but he couldn't have one. Of his three daughters, he had lost one to meningitis in infancy, and the other to a horrific car accident on her way to high school. Since God took two of his daughters by Himself and left one to him, he would think 'God knows best' he would not rebel against Him but would take his anger out of Mrs. Meryem. Although he was not good at showing love, he held on to his only remaining child Füsun, careful not to let go of his authority, and supported her under any circumstances.

When she graduated from Çukurova University Faculty of Medicine, Füsun was assigned to Nevşehir. Her father, who did not want to send her there alone, sent her mother with her and had them rent a house together at the expense of loneliness. Mr. Mustafa and Emin's father, who had been friends since primary school, decided that it would be very suitable to marry their children, both of whom became doctors.

Füsun came back to Adana later and got married to Emin. Emin was twenty-six, and Füsun was twenty-five when they got married. Füsun, a thin, tall, and attractive young girl, impressed Emin straight away. Even though they didn't spend much time in Adana together when they were children, due to Mr. Mustafa's assignments in other cities, Füsun always admired Emin in the rare moments they saw each other in the past. Her desire to be noticed by him and the possibility of becoming his wife one day excited her and always occupied her mind. When the day she waited for arrived and her father told her about the situation, she couldn't believe her ears. They got married in a short time; they had three children. Füsun wanted to raise her children in an authoritarian way, the way her family raised her. Unlike Emin, she was a tough parent with strict rules, but she loved her children very much just like every mother. She wanted them to grow up to be good persons, and she believed that this was possible with strict discipline.

A PERSON'S PERSPECTIVE ON THE WORLD DEPENDS ON WHAT THEY WANT FROM THE WORLD

3) GÜL MEETS ALPER... 1971

Gül saw Alper for the first time when she went to a friend's house when she was studying at the Faculty of Medicine in Izmir. Her high school friend, who was studying law, said,

"We will meet with friends from the faculty on Saturday, you should come too," Gül said to her friend, whom she loved very much and who remained a friend for many years,

"I will come, of course." On that Saturday, the sea breeze that spreads the girl scent of the sea* all over Izmir, together with the sun was carrying the people away. Feeling good with the energy of her youth, Gül had spent extra time on herself that day, took extra care of herself, and looked very beautiful. Even after years, whenever she remembered the memories of the past and the day she met Alper, for some reason, she always remembered the hours she spent to look better.

She would say, "It was as if I had known I was going to go

out with someone, I had a hunch."

When she reached her friend's house and entered through the door, she saw a handsome boy playing baglama and singing. The boy was singing 'Snowy Beech Forest', and he sang it really well. Other young guests were also singing along with him. This song, which all of them knew and sang from heart, had created a magical atmosphere in the room. Gül had sat quietly on the chair next to the door. But she couldn't take her eyes off this black-browed, dark-eyed young man by whom she was immediately impressed. His beautiful voice, his fingers wandering around the strings of the baglama, and his eyes closing occasionally while singing had impressed her.

When the young man finished his little concert and lifted his head, his eyes were met with a pair of eyes that looked at him with interest. He involuntarily smiled at the beautiful girl sitting across from him and looking at him with interest.

"That was beautiful," said Gül, smiling.

"Thank you," said the boy.

"You guys haven't met, have you?" said the owner of the house and introduced them. The name of the boy who played and sang that beautiful folk song was Alper.

At the end of the day, when Alper offered to take her to her home, Gül happily accepted this offer. When they got off to make a bus transfer in Konak, they had walked a long distance on the seashore towards Kordon Boyu, and they had the opportunity to chat in the meantime. Alper liked the intensity of Gül's feelings and her natural reaction to all kinds of beauty and delicacy, her optimism. The softness of her voice also impressed Alper.

The beautiful day they spent at their friends' house, the conversations they had while walking by the seaside on a warm October evening, Alper's shy waving after Gül got on the bus and the happiness Gül felt for meeting Alper was the turning point of the good future for both of them. They would always remember that beautiful day fondly in the future.

Alper and Gül met a few more times and had a great time. As the number of times they met increased, they could not see any reason not to take this further and they had decided to get married. Gül also liked his seriousness, his strong sense of justice, and his good looks. They had a love marriage, from which two daughters were born: Alya and Dila. Shortly after their marriage, before the girls were born, Alper had decided to open a joint law firm with his friend in his hometown, and they settled in Adana together.

Alper, brought up in a patriarchal family with traditional values, was a lawyer who worked hard, and he could not prevent his work from affecting his life, he was in love with his job. He was not very close with his daughters, but he met more than their material needs. He even had to go to the office on many Saturdays and Sundays. Something would come to his mind, he would make an appointment to meet with a client at the office. Naturally, the plans they made to go out for the weekend the night before would fail. Many times, they made a summer vacation plan but they had to postpone it? In a few of those vacations, which they intended to go all together, Alper could not make it due to his works, and Gül had to go only with their daughters.

Gül, on the other hand, was a person who loved to be with her daughters and to spare time for herself while trying to deal with their problems as much as she could.

'Healthy Living Center Fiziform,' where she tried to go regularly after work and spent a lot of time, was one of her *sine qua non*. Her aerobics instructor, Sema, who kept her healthy both physically and mentally, was a friend whom she met outside the center for a drink and heart-to-heart chats.

Occasionally, she would meet with some of her colleagues from work and go shopping or meet and chat over coffee or tea. Gül included what she wanted in her life, finding ways to let off steam. She was a successful physician who worked hard and was loved by the staff and patients.

Alper, on the other hand, did not like meeting his colleagues outside of work; he preferred to spend his evenings relaxing at home. Their perceptions of the world, their stances, their tastes were completely different. These different perspectives on life, which could be tolerated in the first few years of marriage, led to conflicts, resentment, and less tolerance for each other over time. Both had to admit that they were disappointed in what they 'expected' from their spouse.

*A reference to the lines from Cahit Külebi's poem Requiem for Atatürk "The sea smells of girls, girls smell of the sea in Izmir and the streets smell of both girls and the sea".

THERE IS ALWAYS AN ADULT WHO LEAVES A MARK ON THE FUTURE OF CHILDREN

4) CEM AND HIS AUNT GO TO THE DENTIST...
1977

Since Emin thought that spending time with animals had a positive effect on the development of children, he always encouraged his children to stay over at their grandparents' farm when they were little kids. Sometimes Cem's grandfather or uncle would take him to the farm after school because he wanted to go. Although Füsun did not like this at all and complained, Cem would spend days at the farm; he would go there straight from school and go to school from there the next day. The farmhouse, which was on the road to Kozan and fifteen kilometers away from Adana, was a magical world full of all kinds of exploration opportunities for Cem. He would feed the animals at the farm, get information from his uncle about their problems, and memorize the answers to the questions he asked to use the information later. He knew the names and characteristics of all the animals by heart.

"My son will be a veterinarian," would say his grandfather, Mahmut. He picked fruits from the trees and ate them, staying in the garden until late at night, always finding something to discover and learn. The best times of Cem's childhood were spent on that farm.

Especially his great aunt Şengül, who never got married or had her own children and regarded him as her own son, and did everything he asked, had always been his favorite. Cem looked a lot like his father. While his other two siblings had brown eyes like their mother's, Cem's eyes were blue like his father's. He was a tanned boy with dark hair, and there was a glint of gold both on his skin and his hair in summer.

"My handsome son," his aunt would say to him. During the days when Cem stayed at the farm, his aunt did everything to make him happy. There was a special bond between Cem and his aunt.

Cem was nine years old when that event took place, in which his aunt played the leading role, and which would have a great effect on the direction of his future. It was a beautiful Friday afternoon, one of the days when Cem was staying at the farm, and the school was off. There was no one in the house but his aunt and himself; everyone was somewhere else. While his aunt was making lentil meatballs for Cem, who loved food, he was playing with paper ships in the waterways between the plants that he had built in the garden.

He suddenly saw his aunt come out of the house with her hand pressed to the side of her chin, with pain on her face. She shook her head helplessly and looked for Cem with her eyes. Seeing his aunt like that, Cem got up and ran towards her.

"What happened Aunty?" he said in a worried tone.
"It's my tooth Cem, my tooth hurts. I couldn't relieve it no matter what I have done. Come on, get ready we're going to the dentist!" she said with pain.

"Okay, Aunty," said Cem, and quickly went to change his shoes. He was alarmed to see his beloved aunt suffer like that. Even years later, he would never forget how he didn't know what to do and how worried he was for his aunt.

They took the minibus and went to the dental hospital. Even during that short journey, he could not take his eyes off his suffering aunt, he held her hand lovingly and kissed it. His aunt couldn't speak, she was just moaning with her hand on her jaw. For Cem, the road felt like it was getting longer and longer, and every time the minibus stopped, he looked angrily at the boarding passengers, unaware of everything.

Finally, they reached the hospital; they checked in and started to wait in front of the dentist's room. As he saw tears flowing down from his beloved Aunt Şengül's eyes, his eyes filled with tears as well, and he prayed for her pain to be relieved. It was as if he was in pain too. His aunt was waiting, shaking her head from side to side with one hand on her jaw in pain. Luckily, there were not many people waiting. The patient before them came out, and it was their turn when two female guests came for the dentist. The dentist, a handsome young man, signaled Cem and his aunt to wait and took the new guests to his room. His aunt and Cem began to wait. They could hear the sound of conversation and laughter coming from the dentist's room. Time was running and the dentist would not call for his aunt. He was standing up, - because he couldn't sit anymore - walking back and forth, unable to take his eyes off the dentist's door. He was so enraged at the man that he could kill him.

That day, after this painful event, Cem decided to become a doctor and never do what that dentist did. Looking into his aunt's wet, blue eyes, he promised himself that he would help people when they needed him the most, that he would do whatever he could to relieve their pain.

Even years later, he would remember that event and remember his great aunt fondly who made him decide to become a doctor. There would be other events in the future where Cem saw others suffer and promised himself that he would never be the cause of their pain... In fact, because of these promises he made, his destiny would take a different direction...

Cem, who was twelve years old when Emin and Füsun got divorced, lived in Adana for about two more years before high school, but continued to spend most of his days on the farm and commute to school from there. That's how he got away from the unpredictable conflicts he had with his mother and Zeynep at home, and he felt much better there.

As a successful student, Cem went to boarding school with the financial and moral support of his father at Istanbul Boy's High School, where he wanted to study very much.

OUR PERCEPTIONS ARE ALWAYS SELECTIVE

5) BREAKFAST AT THE PHYSICIANS' CLUB ... 1979

In the early days of spring, when Gül and Emin went to the breakfast held by the Medical Chamber at the Physicians' Club, the stifling heat of Adana had not yet begun, and the warm weather prevailed; on that Sunday, they felt that their families might learn their affair for the first time, and they felt excited about it, and also a little embarrassed. The last time they got together and talked before that breakfast, they thought 'Let the chips fall where they may.' They were both tired of what they had been through and the struggle they had to go through. It was as if they were becoming less and less sensitive about what happened and what would happen...

The sun was shining bright and the children were running around on the green grass. More than eighty guests, most of whom were physicians, were talking, laughing, having deep conversations, and some were chasing after their children. Tables for ten to fifteen people were placed on the green grass. Since almost everyone knew each other at the breakfast buffet, no one's place was fixed, everyone was constantly changing seats.

Gül, Alper, and their daughters came to the Physicians' Club later. They were late, by the time they entered through the door, most of the breakfast food was already finished. When they woke up in the morning and were getting ready to go to breakfast, Alper said:

"I don't like the doctors' group at all," which was enough to make Gül angry.

"I don't understand what's your problem with these doctors," she grumbled.

"Usually, they have their nose in the air, and then..." he started to utter the familiar sentences, but then Gül interrupted him saying,

"You don't have to come." Just when Alper had given up going, he couldn't stand that Dila, who was three years old at the time, started to cry and wanted him to come with them, so he left the house to go with them.

For Alper and Gül, being together has become an obligation and a duty for their children. The verbal abuses of his mother-in-law, who she thought had a negative effect on his son from time to time, had become unbearable as well. Alper's mother, Mrs. Melahat, never liked Gül. Her easygoing manner, her inability to properly fulfill her 'wife' duties towards her husband, not following directives, not showing proper respect to her mother-in-law, and responding her 'impudently' instead of being silent when she should keep quiet were unacceptable for Mrs. Melahat. 'Yes, she may be an educated doctor, but she is a woman first and foremost and she should fulfill her duties towards her husband and children.' Perhaps it is not unexpected for a devoted mother, who raised Alper by herself with great difficulty after the death of his father, to feel this way and say these things. What Gül could not stand was that Alper thought that his mother was right, thought the same way, and accepted everything she says without questioning. There had been a lot of moments when they had a crisis at home because of what his mother said to him about her. A person could remain like a little child who listened to every word of their mother even after growing up and becoming an adult. Their marriage was not going well, it would probably end soon. All she thought about was her daughters Alya and Dila and that they would grow up without their father by their side.

As the breakfast at the Physicians' Club carried on, Emin was chatting with his son, looking over at the door. When the Çevik family entered the garden, Emin's eyes were directly focused on Gül. It was impossible not to notice Gül in her yellow dress, with tiny yellow hairpins in her short hair. Emin would later confess to a close friend that the sight of her entering through the garden gate came to his mind from time to time and that made him feel very happy. Emin was answering his son Cem's questions about the features of the engine and components of sports cars. When he turned his head in the direction his father was looking at, he saw Alya, whom he did not like at all and described as 'chubby girl with plain hair,' and he grimaced. He didn't like this girl at all

"Cocky thing!" he said as he went to join his friends, thinking that she would come over to their table, and he didn't come back until the end of the breakfast. Cem was twelve and Alya was eight at that time. Who knew what they would go through years later, how much they would suffer because of the promises they made?

When Alper and Gül came to the table Emin and his family were sitting, Füsun was in the middle of a deep conversation with a friend about her workplace. When she saw them, she jumped up and said to Gül,

"How beautiful you look today," kissing her cheeks. She made room for them to have a seat at the table. Alper and Emin, who had met before, shook hands, said "How are you?" to each other, and sat down. The long breakfast table was too crowded; people were coming, going, sitting, getting up, and chatting with laughter. Everyone, especially children, had a great time in the open air. Emin and Gül did not get tired of looking into each other's eyes at every opportunity they got at that breakfast, which continued late into the afternoon. Their senses were selective, they were able to find the other with their eyes in such a crowd. They gave fleeting glances to each other like teenagers and were happy about it. The sneaking glances, the occasional acceleration of the heart rate, and the desire to be side by side added to their excitement. They both felt special and beautiful.

BEGINNING A NEW LIFE MAY LEAD TO SOMEONE ELSE'S DESTRUCTION

6) EMİN SAYS THAT HE WANTS A DIVORCE... 1979

Of course, Emin and Gül had thought about the difficulties they would face for this affair that had started in spite of themselves. They had failed to play the role of a parent imposed on them by society and knew that they would have to face the judgments, harassments, and gossip of the people in their circles when they declared their affair. When they decided to continue their affair despite everything, they had to let their families know, and that was the hardest part of the whole thing.

Cem had been at the basketball camp outside Adana for four days, and Zeynep wasn't home, she had said the day before,

"I will stay at my friend's house tomorrow", and Yiğit had already fallen asleep. The popular American TV series of then 'Dallas' they were watching on TV had just ended. Füsun had taken the fruit and snack plates to the kitchen, returned to the living room, and she had just sat down when Emin said,

"I want a divorce." Füsun couldn't comprehend it at first.

Thinking he was joking, she was only able to look at his face, and all she could say was "What?". She stared at Emin, waiting for him to say more. Emin was finally able to say the sentence that was most difficult for him to say, the sentence that he had been putting off for days because he didn't know how to say it. He too was looking at Füsun's face, waiting for her reaction.

"I didn't know how to tell you this for a long time, I don't want you to be upset, but that's what I want," said Emin. "But why?" Füsun could only ask. Hundreds of questions were running through her head, but she couldn't ask any of them because she was unable to do so. She just sat for a while, looking at him in shock.

"You know, our marriage is not going well," said Emin. "What's wrong with our marriage?" Füsun asked in a sad voice.

"I don't know about you, but I can't say you met my expectations," said Emin unpleasantly. Füsun lifted her head and looked at Emin's face without saying anything.

"We don't share anything anymore, we are like two strangers in the same house," said Emin.

"What about the children?" Füsun was finally able to say as if the thought had just occurred to her.

"Yiğit is only three years old," she said as if talking to herself.

"Children will never be neglected," said Emin, and he went to the kitchen. Füsun was stuck where she was sitting, unable to move; she felt as if there was a lump in her throat. While Emin entered the room with a beer in his hand, Füsun asked:

"Is there someone else?" looking questioningly at Emin's face. Emin didn't answer, he couldn't, instead, he went to the window and started to look at the dark and silent street. He didn't have the courage to look at Füsun's face. They were both silent for a while, lost in their own thoughts.

Füsun finally found the strength to say,
"Who is that bitch?".

"Gül," Emin said quietly. Füsun's eyes widened. She thought, 'My friend Gül?' and realized that she could not utter that sentence, so instead,

"Gül with whom you go to Mersin?" she asked bitterly. Emin nodded. Jumping to her feet and looking at Emin's back, she said, "I've been feeling the changes in you for a long time. So that's why," sounding like she was talking in her sleep. For a brief moment, there was a silence in the room again.

"God damn you, both of you," Füsun said, with her eyes suddenly filling with tears. She couldn't believe what she heard, she didn't want to believe it. Going back and forth in the room,

"How could you do such a thing?" she attacked this time. She started to cry and badly insult Emin. "What do you expect from a man who doesn't care about his children, could you call him a father?" she cried, hitting Emin on his sore spot. Of course, Gül also got her share from these insults. Emin told Füsun to calm down several times, but this only made Füsun even angrier. Emin merely answered his wife's questions and swallowed up her insults to himself and Gül while drinking his beer in silence with his head bowed.

Füsun wanted to scream with the intense pain in her chest, but she couldn't. It was only with a burst of crying that she was able to reduce her escalating anger. She wept, shuddered, shouted, cried, said whatever came to mind, insulted, and asked questions, before finally calming down. The lampshade she threw with anger was lying on the ground, with its porcelain lower part shattered into pieces, its light bulb still lighting.

Füsun was now crying silently in her armchair, handkerchief in her hand. After some time, Emin was finally able to say,

"We tried hard to end this affair, believe me. We told ourselves that this shouldn't happen, but it was useless. Forgive me, Füsun, please."

"May God forgive you, but know that I never will," said Füsun bitterly. At a moment when Füsun was sitting on the sofa in pain, with her tears ran out, and they had been quiet for some time, Emin left the room saying,

"I'm going to bed, I have work tomorrow, good night." That was it, he had said what he wanted to say and headed for the guest bedroom to sleep.

Füsun loved her husband, her home, and her children very much; it wasn't going to be easy to let go of them and accept what had happened. She was caught off guard, and her pink world, which she had built with hard work, had collapsed when she least expected it. As soon as she was alone in the room, she sank into the chair, deep in thought. Out of many emotions running through her heart, she was unsure which one to feel; but the most intense one was anger. Despite all her yelling and crying, her anger hadn't subsided when Emin was in the room. After he left, she calmed down a bit and tried to think reasonably.

At the end of the night when the night turned into morning, she had to face a lot of emotions besides anger: self-pity, regret, jealousy, pain... So it turns out, she had neglected some things without realizing it while she was divided between her children, husband, home, and work. Things that were important to her in her life were not a priority for her husband, who, despite their children, was able to throw everything away. Füsun thought for a long time that she had to fight this unfair action against her by her dear friend and her husband. What would this fight be like? Would it look like 'No, I'm not getting a divorce, I'm going to make them miserable'? Or would it be not letting Emin see the children? Making the divorce difficult was also an option. All of these required patience, strength, and firmness in the face of what would happen, and Füsun had no energy to deal with any of them. Fighting meant exhaustion.

SOMETIMES LIFE PUTS MORE BURDEN ON YOUR SHOULDERS THAN YOU CAN CARRY

7) FÜSUN IS IN DEPRESSION... 1980

Füsun had a very unhappy and hopeless time during that period and for a few years afterward. Things were not going well either at work or at home; she felt like life was a heavy burden on her shoulders. She felt tired, angry, and cheated.

It was as if she had no purpose in life. She had to force herself to get out of bed in the morning; it took a long time for her to recover. As soon as she got up, she would smoke a cigarette, wander aimlessly around the house with her hair disheveled and start her morning fights with her sleeping children. After sending them to school, she would hurriedly put something on and leave the house. She had gained a lot of weight, she started not to wear make-up and not to go to the hairdresser, which she used to do very often, and stopped looking after herself. Sometimes it was too difficult to even comb her hair.

Füsun, who was the responsible physician at the health center where she worked, started to neglect her work after this unfortunate event. Her mind was always elsewhere and she had a hard time concentrating on anything. She was neglecting necessary correspondences, mostly due to forgetting. The necessary medical supplies for the patients could not be procured on time, which aggrieved the patients. This situation led to a slowdown and disruption in the ongoing work, and worse still, it created conflicts between the patients and the staff, and sometimes arguments became inevitable. Füsun could not update herself because she had difficulty reading and understanding what she needed to read.

Her authority on the employees also suffered from this situation. Wrong decisions she made both in administrative matters and in issues that the staff consulted her were disrupting work and damaging the staff's respect towards her. In face of these undesirable situations and complaints, the Health Directorate had to dismiss her and give the responsibility of the health center to another physician.

At that time, she attributed these negativities to the absence of a husband who supported her. She considered herself 'abandoned' and 'alone.' She believed that if she played the victim, she would become 'a more tolerable person' to those around her. Her confusion was reflected around in the form of anger; most of the time, she was extremely angry and aggressive. Unreasonable fears haunted her.

Employees said something behind her back; their reactions in case of a crisis were,

"Never mind her! She is not herself these days!". When she was alone at night, questions occupied her mind and she could not sleep. She was constantly nervous and worried. She had a hard time coming to terms with what had happened, the storms in her heart affected her children, making their lives unbearable. Füsun had a hard time carrying the responsibility of home, work, and children, all of which suddenly placed on her shoulders, and she had lost her balance and had to seek psychological support for a long period.

Zeynep told her father about the problems she had with the staff at work –because she was constantly whining at home. Emin arranged an appointment for her in another health center by using his current social circle and power in Adana. It was good for Füsun, whose life became very difficult and heavy, to start working in a new place with new people.

Realizing that she needed to be strong for her children, Füsun was able to overcome this bad period with self-affirmations, professional support, and the support she received from her family and friends. Yes, she loved Emin and suffered a lot because of breaking up with him, but 'enough was enough' and she knew that she had to look ahead and think about her children's future...

NOT EVERYONE FEELS THE BURDEN OF LIFE IN THE SAME WAY

8) FÜSUN IS CALLED BY THE SCHOOL FOR ZEYNEP... 1979

After Emin married Gül and moved to Urla, Füsun and the children stayed in Adana and moved to a new place. Zeynep was very fond of her father and she had the hardest time getting over her father's leave. She was angry at her father for abandoning her mother, at her mother for not being able to make her father stay, and at Gül for taking her father away from her...

Zeynep was nine years old when Füsun received a phone call from her school near the end of her shift at work on one day. The caller was the vice-principal and was asking her to stop by the school. Füsun felt that something was wrong when she left the health center to go to school, and she was very nervous. She was anxious on the way about what would happen, she was deep in thought, images from the past with Zeynep in them flashing before her eyes. She was aware that Zeynep's mood had not been stable at all lately. It was normal for any child whose parents got divorced to have a hard time. Zeynep was probably going through such a period.

When the janitor took her to the office of the vice-principal,

Füsun's anxiety got worse when she saw that the form teacher and the school counselor were in the room with the vice principal. Even during the small talk, Füsun had a hard time concentrating and she could hardly hear anything. When the form teacher said,

"Mrs. Füsun, the reason why we called you is that," she held her breath and waited to hear what the issue was. The form teacher continued, "Zeynep has been ill-tempered for the last 3-4 months. Her aggressive behavior towards her friends and teachers has now become unbearable."

She said, "We think that Zeynep should be taken to a psychiatrist with the suggestion of our school counselor." She explained how she had a crying crisis when the math teacher asked her a question in the class the other day, saying,

"My father doesn't love us anymore, he chose someone else's children over us," and how she left the class in anger, saying, "I hate grown-ups." The form teacher said,

"Her classmates don't want to be around her." In fact, the parent of a student with whom she had a problem came to the school to complain, the school administration had hardly calmed the parent down, etc... They were talking about a lot of stuff like this, which infuriated Füsun. She listened angrily to what was told without making any remarks. She knew Zeynep very well and knew that she was capable of doing most of the things she was being told. But she also knew that none of the teachers, who were shedding crocodile tears as if they felt sorry for Zeynep and wanted to help, didn't care, and that most of them were just pretending. She also knew what Zeynep told her about them at home, and she knew that they did nothing to help...

When Füsun left school, she felt exhausted; she also had a headache. On top of all the problems she had, now she had to deal with this too. Of course, this is how Zeynep, who was very fond of her father and was abandoned by him, would react. Füsun was not mentally very well at that time, she was very angry with the teachers who did nothing to help her child. Yes, there were times when she thought that Zeynep should get psychiatric support, but she couldn't find the strength in herself to take action about it, so she had postponed it. But the situation was serious now and she had to act immediately.

Füsun had to make a lot of effort to explain to Zeynep that she needed to go to the doctor properly and to get her to accept it. Her daughter kept screaming that she wasn't insane. Yes, Zeynep would have to be taken to a psychiatrist and had to take psychotherapy and medication.

Problems she would face in her academic and private life, and moreover, in her relationships with people, would lead her to take refuge in colors, brushes, and drawing papers. Drawing pictures and working with paints would be a safe haven for her to find the strength to endure what she goes through, to add color to her life, and calm the storms.

LOVE BLOOMS BY ITSELF AS PEOPLE GET TO KNOW EACH OTHER

9) SUMMERS SPENT IN URLA... MATURING PERSONALITIES...

After Gül and Emin got married, they moved to Urla. Almost every summer, all children would spend the summer in this house with a large garden in Urla. These 'summer meetings' would allow them to get to know each other better, continue their relationship in the future, and leave a mark on all of them in one way or another.

Zeynep was ten years old when she first saw the house where her father and Gül lived. It was hard to accept at first, yes, but she eventually loved Urla, the big house with the pool and the garden. She also had a room that she shared with Yiğit. After all, Gül and her daughters had taken her father away; so she was capricious and moody at first. If it was up to her, she would never go there, but the insistence of her mother, who did not want Yiğit to go alone, her longing for her father, and the jealousy she felt towards Gül's daughters would also make her go back every year. To the extent of her observations with her parents and their married friends, there were always quarrels between married couples. She was wondering if similar quarrels between her parents in the past would happen between Gül and her father as well, and her curiosity was taking her back there as well. When she wanted to be alone, she would do her favorite activity there too: she would go to her room and paint.

But as the years passed by and they all grew up and got more mature, their thoughts of each other would become softer and they would have more tolerance and love for each other. By the end of the summer, photos would be taken, books would be exchanged, and birthdays would be celebrated. Cem and Dila's birthdays were in summer. Zeynep would give away the paintings she made during the summer to the family when it was time to say goodbye. Since she didn't have a sister, she liked to treat them like elder sisters and enjoy the advantages of having a sister. They, too, liked to treat her as a little sister and do whatever she asked for. Zeynep had personally witnessed over the years that her father and Gül loved each other very much; she painfully realized that what her parents lacked in their marriage was respect, which made the marriage of her father and Gül strong...

From the beginning, Cem never wanted to go to his father's new house. He went there for a few summers as a kid, but then he didn't want to go. When he had to be in Urla, he didn't stay at home, he was usually out with friends. He didn't like the idea of spending time with Aunt Gül, and her daughters and Zeynep's whims were unbearable to him. Instead of being with his father's new family, he preferred to spend his summer vacations abroad or with his aunt in Adana...

Yiğit, on the other hand, always loved that place and being there until adolescence; especially the breakfasts on Saturdays and ice creams they had afterward... He would remember going to sea with his father after he came from work and the sandcastles they built with Dila for the rest of his life, and he would painfully realize that those were the best years of his life after the disasters that befell him. He would love Dila, with whom his path would cross from time to time even as adults, and who would always have a special place in his life, even more than his own siblings...

When Emin's children began to enter their family, Dila, the youngest daughter of Gül, also loved all the children, especially Yiğit. Dila and Yiğit were born only three months apart anyway. Being a person of good faith and having a humanistic character, Dila was always happy when she was with them. The feeling that she would always feel intensely, that upset her and that she believed would never go away as she grew a bit older, was longing for her father. Despite this, her stubbornness would prevail, she would put another plan into action, and she would successfully carry it out...

Alya loved that Uncle Emin's children would come from Adana during the summer vacations and the house would get crowded. After all, Uncle Emin was their father and it was their right to be with their father. She even liked Zeynep, even though she was very harsh from time to time and hurt and upset the folks at home. Alya always liked and respected Zeynep's self-confidence and how she would always stick to what she knows is right, defend herself to the end, and how she took Yiğit under her wing. Zeynep was a harsh person but Alya remembered that she made an effort to get along with her and make her happy. After many years, Alya would always say that she saw in Zeynep the importance of 'defending your rights' and 'showing it through behavior' and that Zeynep had greatly affected her own personality. Alya had kept most of the paintings that Zeynep had given to her before returning to Adana, and she had some of them framed and hung on the walls of her house. Especially, the painting of a house and a tree that she liked to see on the bedroom wall very much was her favorite, she always hung this painting on the wall in every house she moved.

While they were all together, Gül tried to take care of both her children and Emin's children; she did her best to keep the relations among them warm. Cem, Zeynep, and Yiğit called her 'Aunt Gül' and they loved her very much. Although Zeynep was angry and overreacted to her, even she loved her even though she didn't realize it.

Gül knew what the children liked and didn't like; she would make her domestic plans by considering those issues. Gül was the person who started Saturday breakfasts that almost became traditional. The place they usually went to was the Submarine Cafe next to the Tanju Okan Park, located by the sea. She did her best to make the children comfortable. She would try to start a conversation about the topics all of them were interested in, tell them positive things and try to entertain them all. Sometimes there would be such laughter at their table that Emin had to warn them that people at the tables around them may be disturbed by their noise. To jump into the sea in the cool waters of Kalabak Beach with the swimsuits they wore underneath their clothes after eating their ice cream, to continue having fun there and spending the day in this way were the first memories they remember from the Saturday activities they had in Urla, which always made them smile with love... Gül would think that the world was beautiful and it should never change as she was watching outside from the window of the living room, and the sycamore trees along the driveway, and she would thank God for her healthy and happy family.

Emin, on the other hand, would happily support Gül's efforts to make the children comfortable when his children come along during the summer vacations. He appreciated how successful Gül was in crisis management when there were problems among the children, and how she handled the problems very smoothly in some cases. Emin had seen the family relations, communications, and the steps taken with good intentions and was proud of Gül for always treating his children well.

Emin thought that the most remarkable thing about the Başar and Çevik siblings, who spent their summers together, was that they did not hate each other. On the other hand, it didn't seem like they were attached to each other.

But in the first years of their marriage, the only problem that preoccupied Emin's mind was usually Zeynep. When they would go somewhere together with the children, the little ones would happily have fun; Zeynep, on the other hand, would take pleasure in very few things, she would always grumble and want to return home. He thought that the reason for these capricious behaviors was her jealousy and he was hoping that they would decrease over time. After all, Zeynep was just a child.

During their time together, just when Zeynep's prejudices about Gül and her daughters would be about to end, just when she would be close to feeling comfortable with them, the summer would be over, and she would return to Adana with her brother. Emin saw that she became a little more mature and harmonious in each summer vacation that followed. Years later, Zeynep would confess to her boyfriend that she had the most memorable moments of her life there…

Over the years, as children grow up, get emotionally matured, and start to think reasonably and positively, all memories, except the ones they can't erase or make a special effort not to erase, get erased from their memory and become forgotten. A growing person gets to know people better, evaluates their worldview, stance, and perspective better, and loves them if they think they are worthy of love. They had started to get to know each other starting from an early age by coming together during the summers. They had figured out whether they were family or rivals, by being torn between different emotions, but they had all figured it out differently.

YOU NEED TOLERANCE TO BE HAPPY

10) YİĞİT LOSES THE KEY TO THE CAR… 1981

Yiğit, who was very fond of cars when he was little, would sometimes take his father's car key; he loved to hold it in his hand and pretend he was putting it in the ignition. Whether inside or outside the house, when he got the key, he would put it in the ignition of a car in his imagination and start the car. He would take a ride on the roads, again in his imagination, making the sound of a motor with his throat. This was an enactment that Yiğit, a child with a big imagination, created by himself and did whenever he got a car key.

On a beautiful Sunday morning when the sun was warming, Emin, who was working as a physician in a private hospital, was on duty for twenty-four hours, and Gül and Yiğit went to the hospital to pick up Emin because his car was in maintenance. Yiğit was five years old at the time, he woke up early that day, and when he asked,

“Can I come with you to pick up dad?” Gül couldn't resist, so she said, “Of course, you can come!” and took him with her. After they picked up Emin from the hospital, on the way back.

AGGRESSION IS SOMETIMES A CRY FOR ASKING HELP

11) DILA'S DOLL... 1983

On a hot Saturday in Urla, Emin could not resist Zeynep and Yiğit's insistence and took them to swim as he promised. Gül, who felt bored with house chores and wanted a little change of air, went to Izmir with her daughters Alya and Dila.

It was the third year of their marriage; Alya was eleven and Dila was seven. Their grandmother, who loved and missed her grandchildren very much, was surprised when she saw them all. They had a great time, and after they hungrily ate the flour cookies and the bulgur salad their grandmother made for them, they went to the historical Kemeraltı Bazaar together. They wandered around Kemeraltı and shopped. Gül bought Latife Tekin's latest novel 'Dear Cheeky Death,' a doll for Dila, and a colorful and decorated diary for Alya.

Their main purpose for going to Kemeraltı was to go to Şan Cinema to watch Flashdance, a musical movie that was popular all over the world at the time, starring Jennifer Beals and Michael Nouri. When the movie ended and they left the cinema, all three had a great time and felt very happy. The dance scenes in the romantic movie, which are considered Hollywood classics from the 1980s by cinephiles, had fascinated them all. Also, the original soundtrack of the movie, 'Flashdance... What a Feeling" would be awarded the Academy Award for Best Music, and the stirrup leggings would become a fashion trend after this movie...

After the movie, Dila, who was seven years old at the time, said,

"I decided to be a dancer when I grow up." Gül welcomed this decision of Dila, who had a thinner body and longer legs than Alya's, with a smile, and replied,

"Why not, that would be amazing." But the future would not bring what they had hoped, Dila's path would be very different, not even close to performing arts such as dance or ballet...

Going back to Urla that evening, Gül and her daughters all sat in a corner in the living room, resting after a long day. Dila was playing with her new doll, and Alya was watching TV. While Gül was sitting on the blue armchair in the corner with the book she had just bought, Emin and his children came home. Zeynep entered the hall, shouting and clamoring; she was very angry and was storming mad.

Without greeting anyone, she was heading to the stairs and quickly went up. Following Zeynep, Emin and Yiğit entered the hall, silently looking at her. Everyone in the room was holding their breath, watching. Especially Alya and Dila were watching her with wide-eyed fear. They all followed her with their eyes as she was climbing up the stairs. When she slammed her door with a loud noise, Dila jumped in her seat in fear and turned her eyes to her elder sister. Alya reached out and pulled her close, wrapping her arms around her neck and silently saying,

"Don't be afraid." Zeynep was having one of her usual nervous breakdowns; she would suddenly get angry, shout, and wouldn't care about anything or anyone. They were used to her attitude by now. In this situation, Emin and Gül would feel helpless. Yiğit went next to the girls and sat in the three-seater; he joined them and started watching TV. Emin, on the other hand, sat on the other armchair next to Gül, shook his head, ran his hands helplessly through his hair, and fell into deep thought.

"What's the issue?" Gül asked quietly. Emin looked at the children on the sofa, staring intently at the television.

"We'll talk later," he said.

They were all upset about the situation. They watched TV in silence and spoke little for the rest of the evening until it was time for bed.

Dila, who heard the sound of music coming from Zeynep's room as she was going to bed, wanted to show her doll to Zeynep and went into her room.

Zeynep, who was still angry, started screaming,

"I don't want to see your doll or you; leave me alone, get out of my room!" and kicked Dila out of her room. When everyone retired to rest in their rooms at night, Emin said to his wife,

"I am worried about Zeynep a lot," looking at Gül with despairing eyes.

"I think she's still angry with me and she's very unhappy," he added. That day, she had done everything to disturb them, caused incidents for trivial reasons, was unsatisfied with everything. Their day had not gone as they had hoped at all. Gül said.

YOU MAY REALIZE A DIFFERENT FACE OF A PERSON YOU THINK YOU KNOW

12) THE FIRST BIG FIGHT... 1985

Gül and Emin met in front of the restaurant where they had a reservation to enjoy the sunset and have dinner after work. Since they got married and settled in Urla five years ago, drinking raki and eating seafood has been one of the most enjoyable activities for both of them. Before the dark blue dusk of Izmir, they decided to swim in the sea to relax a bit. The sun was about to set in Ildırı, a virgin, untouched village where technology had not yet entered. As soon as they immersed themselves in the water, they felt peace surrounding their entire bodies. The redness of the sunset on their faces, the fishing boats gliding gracefully on the sea around them, the shadows of the trees on the small hills around the sea looked magnificent. The happiness and love in their eyes were worth seeing as they swirled together facing each other with the halo of the sun swirling around their heads. There was nothing around them except for the boats. It was so quiet that when they spoke, their voices echoed off the tiny hills around them that were right by the sea.

If they had raised their voices slightly, someone not far

away from the shore would have been able to hear them. The sea was so clear that long, dark green seaweed clumps at the bottom, and the fish swimming softly among the seaweeds could easily be seen.

They chatted there side by side in the sea, sometimes splashing each other with water, sometimes getting into deep conversations, sometimes racing each other while swimming. They told such things to each other that there were moments when they could not control their laughter. Emin's laughter, which was very loud, echoed in the bay and it filled them with even more happiness. They had not felt so carefree for a long time, like young lovers.

The time flew by, and it was getting dark. Despite being in the sea for so long, neither of them felt like getting out of the water. The glow of the sun that was about to set changed the color of their eyes, and they couldn't get enough of looking into each other's eyes. Both were aware that this was a rare moment. They hugged each other tightly to enjoy that moment together and neither of them wanted to let go.

How happy they were in this place where the sea was within walking distance. Get out of work, go to the sea, take a few strokes, go home, have dinner, and rest... It was wonderful to live there. When they finally realized that they were hungry, they got out of the water. After taking a shower, they got dressed in casual clothes and sat at a table in the shabby fish restaurant. Emin couldn't take his eyes off Gül, who looked great in her majestic white dress, which suited her tanned skin very well.

The dinner started well. They were sipping their drinks, accompanied by fried shrimp, feta cheese, tomatoes, and cucumbers. They had not yet ordered fish, they were chatting softly. The touching voice of Müzeyyen Senar filled the restaurant, which had wooden walls and tables on the sand and allowed walking down the sea with a couple of steps:

I do not complain to anyone, I cry to myself,

I quiver with fear like a criminal as I look at my future,

The curtain of gloom has been pulled on my luck, I'm afraid.

They remained silent for a while and listened to the song with happiness. They were still feeling the happiness of being alone in the sea and feeling each other. The children were all somewhere else. In the summer, the house was always crowded, and the moments when they could be alone were limited. They wanted to make the most of those moments. As the hours passed by, the food had been eaten, the conversation had deepened, and the second glasses of raki had just ended, Emin said something that made Gül very angry:

"I intended to tell you for a long time, but didn't have the opportunity to, I don't like you being so intimate with Erhan," he said.

"Excuse me?" said Gül, knitting her brows.

"What do you mean intimate?" she continued.

"I mean, close. I don't like it when you are hand in glove and laugh together," said Emin taking a sip from his drink.

"What do you suggest we do, Mr. Emin? I'll act accordingly," she said as she leaned her head towards Emin.

"It makes me uneasy that he gets so close to you and you give him the opportunity to do so," Emin said. Gül fixed her eyes on Emin's eyes, and said,

"Opportunity? What are you talking about, for God's sake! Do you even hear yourself? " she asked sternly, staring into Emin's eyes as if waiting for an answer. Continuing to look at him,

"Besides, Erhan is your friend and you introduced him to me," she said sternly.

"Maybe. But you don't have to be that intimate with him," said Emin. Gül couldn't believe her ears.

"Do you realize you're accusing me of something ugly?" she continued, trying not to raise her voice. Emin was silent, turning his head towards the sea. Gül continued,

"What you're saying is an insult to me and I will accept such a thing!".

"I know Erhan's remarks and thoughts about women, especially beautiful women," Emin spoke again.

"This is not my problem, and it does not concern me at all. I am who I am, and I will not change my behavior according to someone else's request and warning!" said Gül.

"You misunderstood me, I just wanted to warn you about Erhan," said Emin, changing his tune. But Gül was still angry. With her hands on the table, reaching towards Emin, she continued in an angry voice,

"I'm a grown woman and I don't need warnings! Especially warnings made in this way" "Please Gül, I only said it for the best..."

"I want to go home, I don't want to hear anything more!" said Gül, as she got up and headed for the restroom. While she was there, Emin paid the check and began to wait for her by the car. They didn't speak until they got home. The night had started so beautifully with the sunset and ended like this long after the sun was gone. Actually, Gül did not feel anything even slightly negative about Erhan, and she was someone who could put her foot down the moment she felt such a thing. She didn't need anyone's warning about something like this.

Emin would have to make a lot of effort to talk her round, to 'explain what he really meant' and express his actual intention and feelings, and he would succeed in convincing Gül after a few days. Although he was an educated person, in the end, this was Emin's point of view in such matters. He was raised in a patriarchal family and his personality was influenced by the 'male-dominated society'. Even though he had no such thought or purpose, it was always the woman who had to tidy herself up; that's what Gül couldn't stand. Similar conflicts with Gül, who was an independent and free woman, would always occur at various levels throughout their relationship. But they would remember this event as the first and biggest fight they had since they got married.

LITTLE TRAUMAS LEAVE DEEPER MARKS ON LITTLE SOULS

13) HER FATHER BUYS A BEAUTIFUL GIFT FOR DİLA... 1985

When Emin and Gül got married, Dila was a lovely 4-year-old child and was very fond of her father; she grew up longing for him until high school. She learned to say 'Uncle Emin' from Alya, who addressed Emin in that way. Emin, who loved Dila very much, used to call her 'Miss Dila', referring to the movie starring Türkan Şoray and Kadir İnanır.

Dila had a hard time accepting that they had left her father in Adana and moved to Izmir, and could not understand why they were doing such a thing, and constantly questioned why. As she was just a child, she thought that the reason she was apart from him was Emin and her mother who couldn't resist him, so she blamed them. When her anger towards them surfaced from time to time, she made a scene for trivial reasons and went into crying fits; she had always upset Gül by being capricious and stubborn, and she thought that she was taking her revenge in this way. It was not a coincidence that these crises exploded, especially on days she spoke to her father on the phone. For that reason, she always loved the times when Emin was on duty at the hospital because she had more opportunity to be with her mother and she felt that she was all hers and her sister's.

As the years passed by and Dila grew older, she began to have difficulties in properly expressing herself. She was trying to solve the problems on her own, becoming more and more withdrawn because of the little traumas that hurt her sensitive soul. Her stubbornness would also mature along with her, and she would grow up to have a stubborn personality. In the house in Urla, 'Dila's stubbornness' was going to be one of the issues that would come up frequently and angered family members…

Dila started to insist that she wanted to go to Adana during the semester break of the third grade in elementary school. Thinking that she was too young, Gül made a lot of effort to talk her into giving up this idea but she failed to persuade her daughter, who was very insistent about it. Eventually, she had to give up and allowed her to go for a week. Emin had a great influence on this decision, saying that 'she has the right to see her father and spend time with him as well.'

It was that February break when she went to Adana and her father bought her a tiny pair of red butterfly-shaped golden earrings. They went out on that Saturday to have some father-daughter time. Even though it was winter, the sun, which always shone in the sky in Adana, was shining brightly and warming their hearts. Her father's new wife Sevinç couldn't come with them due to a charity bazaar event she had to attend, and had told them,

"Why don't you, as a dad and daughter team, enjoy Adana?" First, they ate kebab and drank turnip juice at a kebab restaurant they regularly visited; after they left the restaurant, they held hands and started walking. Dila regretted that her mother and sister were not there as she walked silently and thoughtfully with her hand in her father's palm. She used to miss her father when she was in Urla, now she miss her mother here.

Dila wanted to go to the cinema after dinner and Alper fulfilled this request. They bought tickets for a science fiction movie that would always have a special place in Dila's life. They watched the movie 'Back to the Future' together at Arı Cinema, a movie in which Doctor Brown built a car that made time travel possible, and they liked it very much. Even as an adult, Dila would always remember that day whenever she saw that movie, how she walked hand in hand with her father on the streets of Adana, and how it made her heart sink whenever her mother came to her mind.

When they entered the Jewelers' Bazaar while walking on Atatürk Street, Alper said,

"Come, my daughter," and took her into the jewelry store. The shop window was filled with gold jewelry, gleamed and dazzled under the bright light bulbs. The owner of the shop, who was a close friend of his father, had that hospitality peculiar to Adana; he was very happy to see Alper and his little daughter and warmly welcomed them to the leather armchairs. After inquiring about each other's health, he asked how he can help them and offered juice to Dila and tea to her father. While his father and his friend were chatting, Dila stood in front of the display counter with the juice bottle in her hand, immersed in her own world, admiring the various golden rings, bracelets, and necklaces.

She snapped out of her thoughts by her father's voice saying, "Dila, let's pick one." When the jeweler asked what she would like, she excitedly replied,

"Earrings." Because she and her mother had just had her ears pierced that summer, she liked earrings the most. The jeweler looked at Dila, smiling, took the tray with dozens of different earrings out of the display counter, and put it in front of her. Surprised, Dila raised her eyebrows and looked at her father, who said,

"You can get whichever you want." Dila was very happy, she excitedly turned her face to the earring tray and began to examine them. After hesitating for a while between the options, she finally picked the butterfly-shaped earring with a yellow body and red stone wings. The jeweler supported her choice, saying,

"You picked a very beautiful one, you are a tasteful girl."

Her father purchased it and helped her put it on, and they came out of the store with her new earring on her ears.

When it got dark in the evening and they returned home, Sevinç excitedly welcomed Alper and his daughter, who had a wonderful day. She asked Dila questions to start a conversation, listened attentively as she talked about what they had done with her father that day, and she said she too liked the earring that they had bought.

During her stay there, her father and wife hosted Dila very well. She had a great time there. When her five-day vacation ended and it was time to return to Urla, Sevinç gifted her a turtleneck sweater with one cream sleeve and one blue sleeve, which Dila would always wear fondly.

One morning, Dila decided to go to school with her new earrings, shortly after she returned to Urla and the end of February holiday. She wanted to show them to her friends; let them see and ask, she wanted to say that they were a 'gift from my dad.' She especially wanted her closest friend Ceren to see them. Because Ceren's father would always buy something for her and whenever she proudly said, "my father bought this for me", which would make Dila's heart sink. She had a father too, and of course, her father could buy her something as well.

The day she put on her earrings, her first class was music and the teacher was a woman whom nobody liked, who used violence against children, and who always shouted. Her name would never be erased from her mind even after many years: Mahire Pekmezci...

She was someone who never smiled at children, didn't say a good word, and probably didn't like children at all. How could someone be a teacher of an art branch and inflict violence on children? There was no way to understand this. She could easily hit the children on the head with a notebook if they made mistakes while playing the flute, and bang the heads of two students to each other if she saw them talking during the class. For this reason, Dila always preferred painting as an elective course throughout her school life, and she stayed away from music courses as much as possible. The nights before the music class would torture Dila, she would lose sleep whenever she thought about that class the next day. A movie she watched as a child could make her want to become a dancer and dance to music in the future, while another event that deeply affected her could make her distance herself from music.

The teacher in question saw her earring during the first class in the morning, and after giving a speech about not coming to school with earrings, she asked her to take them off immediately. Dila did what the teacher told her, who put fear in her heart, took off the earrings, put them in the pocket of her cardigan, went to classes in the morning, never even thought of the earrings for the rest of the morning, and completely forgot about them. Until that event that reminded her, they were there...

Excited to go to the theater that afternoon, Dila had already forgotten what happened in the music class. On that cold March day, when the weather was freezing cold, the whole class ate their lunch excitedly before going to Izmir State Theatre, and then they got on the bus that would take them to the theater under the supervision of their teachers. The two buses lined up in front of the theater and then they went inside.

They had just taken their seats when the play they had

excitedly been waiting for began. The play was great, they were all watching with great attention. The first act of the play was about to end when Dila felt hot and needed to take off her cardigan. Without taking her eyes off the stage, the sound of metal hitting the wood of the chair she was sitting on as she hastily took off her cardigan made her come to her senses and she remembered the earrings. When she checked her pockets, she noticed that the earrings were not there, she had a terrible shock.

She impatiently waited for the break, and she couldn't concentrate on the play as she was thinking about what she could do about it. She had warned her friends about her earrings falling on the floor when the curtain fell. They all looked together between the seats, but they couldn't find them. Most of the children had heard Dila's problem, but they did not even take it seriously. Most of them were chatting among themselves, some of them were criticizing the play and talking all the time.

Dila could not find her earrings because of the crowd, the dim light in the theater, and limited time during the break. She was very upset and cried for hours on the way back to school, and despite the intense efforts of her teachers, it was not possible to calm her down. She had never been able to wear those earrings, and she would never have the heart to tell her father that she lost them.

Later on, whenever she went to the theater, she would always remember those earrings and that music teacher she hated all her life...

YOU MAY HAVE TO MAKE SACRIFICES TO PREVENT THE WOUND YOU HAD IN YOUR CHILDHOOD FROM BLEEDING IN YOUR ADULTHOOD

14) FÜSUN PREPARES FOR A NEW BEGINNING WITH İLKER... 1986

It was the year that Cem got into university and went to Istanbul, and Zeynep started high school. Yiğit was nine years old. Füsun had partially settled her life and continued on her life with a daily routine. She was solving her problems, or rather she was trying to solve them. She had left behind the divorce period, which she thought was the biggest disaster in her life and the period of crying and whining. When she met İlker, her self-care was almost back to normal. Füsun was a smart woman who knew that she had to look ahead for her children and that they had a long life ahead of them. Now her current problems were Zeynep's puberty, which they had to deal with at home together.

At the time of the divorce, the court had ruled that Emin should pay child support for the kids, and Emin was paying the alimony regularly. Believing that she should be careful with her spending, Füsun had moved from the house where she and Emin had lived to a smaller house right after the divorce. At first, there were no problems with the new house, but as the children grew up, they started to complain. Zeynep, who shared the same room with Yiğit as a child, had stated that she did not want to share the same room with him anymore and had raised the flag of rebellion. Füsun was tired of Zeynep's whining. Yiğit was not happy at all with sharing the same room with Zeynep either. The kitchen window facing the air well, which made her exasperated when sipping coffee or cooking, was depressing her as well. Both the desire to make her children happier and the belief that a change of place would be good for them led Füsun to buy a new house.

It had been about six years since she got divorced when she met İlker, a civil engineer, as she was looking for a new house. Füsun was still an attractive forty-four-year-old woman. İlker, on the other hand, was fifty years old, a contractor, a divorcee, and had two children.

During the purchase period of the house that Füsun liked, she had to stop by İlker's office a lot. İlker, who felt that he liked Füsun during these round-trips, tried to get her attention; he tried very hard to make her notice that he liked her with his glances and compliments. He had insisted for a long time to go to dinner together when she came by the office and by calling her house frequently. Füsun, who didn't think such an affair for a mother of three, initially resisted a lot. After some time, when she started to feel a stir in her emotions towards him, she thought a dinner meeting wouldn't hurt anyone and told İlker,

"It's just dinner," surrendered to him.

For the first time in a long time, Füsun was meeting someone who made her heart beat faster. Their dates, which were infrequent at first, became more frequent over time. They went out for dinner and went to the movies a few times. As time passed by, they realized that they got along very well. They were both adults who had left some things behind and were aware that they now had to look ahead to the future. İlker was very kind to Füsun, giving importance to her thoughts, asking for her opinion in any situation, and reminding her that she was important for him at every opportunity. İlker was a charming and humorous person, he did not take life too seriously and could make friends with people from any walk of life. He made Füsun laugh a lot with his jokes. Füsun had not been this happy in a very long time. They had started to see each other more often, share more things.

İlker had started to say, "Marry me!" He had also found a beautiful house suitable for Füsun and her children, which was about to be finished. And he imagined that he would live in that house too - with the hope that it would happen in the future. It was a house built by a contractor friend of his, Kazım, and the children loved it when they saw it. Füsun, who thought that it would be more advantageous to buy a house during the construction phase, started the payments immediately.

When she bought the house, they told her that it was almost finished, but it just kept dragging on. Although he was a good friend of İlker, he wouldn't say anything about the prolonged construction. So Füsun continued to pay money and was looking forward to the day she could move into her new house. Füsun had gone to Kazım's office several times to talk and realized that the man was drunk. When she told about this to İlker, he didn't give much thought to it.

He said, "He might be drunk my dear, we cannot interfere with the man's drink."

As time passed by, Füsun and İlker's affair got more serious and they started to make serious decisions about their future together. Füsun was waiting for the right time to talk to her children and tell them about this relationship. Only İlker's vulnerability for alcohol worried Füsun. Whenever she brought up this subject and asked him about it, İlker got angry.

He would say, "You're hurting my feelings, you're accusing me wrongly." Although he claimed that he did not drink much and that he drank alcohol occasionally and only on special occasions, Füsun was not convinced and suspected that he was drinking almost every evening, praying that her suspicion did not turn out to be true.

One evening, Zeynep and Yiğit went to bed early, right after they had their dinner. Füsun, who herself was dozing off on the sofa, was startled by the ringing of the phone. Thinking, 'Who could this be at this hour?' she went to the phone and picked up the receiver. The caller was İlker, he said,

"Sorry it's so late, but I want to extend an invitation."

"What invitation?" asked Füsun, then she sadly realized that İlker was mumbling.

"I am invited to a dinner at İnci Hotel tomorrow night, I would be very happy if you could join me," said İlker.

"Who will attend the dinner?" Füsun asked.

"Those who influence the construction industry," said İlker. After a few seconds of silence and some thought, Füsun said,

"Okay, I'll come," as her hatred for alcohol, and how much the man she loved liked drinking made her worry about the future, which upset her... Füsun, who had not attended with him to this kind of dinner before, thought that this would allow her to see things more clearly tomorrow. She went to the bedroom to go to bed, thinking anxiously, 'Let's see what God has in store, He knows best.'

She picked what she will wear that night, and went to the hairdresser the next day at noon. İlker, who picked her up from her house in the evening, opened his eyes wide like a child when Füsun got in the car.

"Wow! How beautiful you look!" he said; his surprise made Füsun laugh. The night went very well; Füsun had the opportunity to meet people in İlker's circle. They danced more than they had ever before, they laughed as they had never laughed before. The only problem was that she noticed that İlker drank alcohol like water, and she had to warn him, "Slow down." İlker, on the other hand, tweaked her on the cheek and said,

"Don't worry! Everything is under control!" mumbling as before. For the first time in a long time, Füsun felt this happy. She had broken her chains and thought that she had a right to be happy, which was reflected in her behavior. The woman who cared about what others would think was gone, replaced by a woman who believed that she should live her life and be comfortable from now on.

When it was time to leave the hotel at the end of the night, Füsun saw that İlker was too drunk to stand up. She had suddenly recalled her childhood, and remembered how her father, who would get blind drunk, shouted and broke things. She remembered her father's flashing eyes, his scowling look, and the fear, anger, and embarrassment she felt seeing him like that.

For as long as she could remember, she hated men who lost control after drinking. It was the first time she attended such a dinner with plenty of alcohol, witnessing that İlker had to lean on her to be able to stand. Other things she witnessed while waiting for their car in front of the hotel were his loud cries and obscene curses towards the valet because he was late. Hearing all this, Füsun could not believe her ears, and her eyes filled with tears.

They had drunk alcohol at dinners they had before too, but this was the first time Füsun saw him this drunk. İlker's friend Kazım, the contractor of the new house, which would cost Füsun much more than it actually did, was also at the same dinner, and he was blind drunk as well. Seeing him that way too, Füsun painfully thought that she and other people who were impatiently waiting for the apartment to be finished were most likely paying for his drinks. She actually knew that you cannot do business with people who drink too much alcohol and you should stay away from them and that they would lose touch with reality and make wrong decisions...

That night and those experiences made Füsun question her relationship. She knew she could never be with someone who drinks like that. She remembered her mother, who had to deal with her father when he drank too much and was sometimes physically abused by him, and the possibility of going through the same things scared her a lot.

She decided that she would not go through the same things. She went to İlker's office the very next day. İlker, who wasn't aware of anything, said,

"You were amazing last night!" trying to hug and kiss her, but Füsun prevented him from kissing her by putting her hands on her cheeks and pushing him away. She crossed her arms and said to İlker, who was looking at her questioningly, "Sit down, we need to talk." She asked İlker to listen without interrupting, and she told him all her thoughts and feelings: She could not stand people who lost themselves after drinking a lot, people like her father; she didn't want to have the same fate as her mother; she wants someone in the house who can set an example for her children; the amount of alcohol would always increase over time; she wanted to spend her old age with someone in their right mind... Füsun said whatever came to mind.

While she was speaking, she silenced İlker, who was trying to interrupt and speak, several times by raising her hand. When she finished, İlker's efforts to stop her were futile, and she took her purse and left. Later, İlker begged a lot, tried to change her mind, promised not to drink a single drink again, but all in vain. Füsun had seen all of these in the past, and she had witnessed firsthand that these kinds of promises were never kept. The first affair Füsun after the divorce,

Füsun broke all ties with İlker without mercy and buried her love in her heart in the first incident, thus her first affair after the divorce ended in this way before even starting, and she would not have any other serious affairs for the rest of her life.

She would be relieved that she had a narrow escape, and Emin would be relieved in the same way who found out that her affair with İlker had ended.

Füsun had made some mistakes in her youth but she shaped her life by learning from her mistakes as she matured; she was always strict with herself and always spared little time for herself. Unfortunately, an unexpected death would take Füsun, who always put her children's future before her own happiness and who lived for them, away from the world...

SOMETIMES AN ESCAPE IS A REBELLION

15) ALYA LEAVES URLA... 1986

Alya, the eldest daughter of Gül and Alper, was a plump and quiet child with straight hair falling over her shoulders and with her green eyes hidden behind her glasses. She loved to study, preferred books over people, and created an opportunity to read any time under any circumstance. She had read the three-volume Les Misérables by Victor Hugo, which was over two thousand pages, while she was still in secondary school. She was also a very reasonable person. Her closest and best friends were animals, especially dogs, and she shared her loneliness and home with them in every period of her life.

When Emin and Gül got married and settled in Urla, Alya and her sister Dila left Adana, left their friends and school behind, and started living in Urla. They enrolled in a school there too, but Alya did not like her new school. The difference between Alya and Dila was that Alya cared about things. Alya cared about authors, animal rights, justice, and even her grades from the classes she didn't like. She cared about what their mother said about their father. Dila, on the other hand, wanted to either withdraw to her room and read Barbara Cartland or watch the popular TV show 'Blue Moon', 'Tree of Life' or 'Love Boat'.

Their mother's new husband, Uncle Emin, was a really nice person and treated her and her sister very well, but Alya didn't like living in the same house with someone she called 'uncle' instead of her father. As she grew older, she started to get bored in Urla, much more bored during the winter. Alya was a successful student and wanted to go to high school in İzmir, she got into Güzelbahçe 60th Year Anatolian High School. They were very happy when she got accepted into this school, but her grandmother was the happiest of them all, saying,

"I am very happy my granddaughter will live with me!". The school was in Izmir and it was very close to Urla. She usually stayed with her grandmother in İzmir on weekdays, sometimes even on weekends when she did not want to go back to Urla. She only went back there when she missed her mother and sister a lot. When Uncle Emin's children came to Urla during the summer vacations, she would be there too.

IF YOU HAVE NOBODY TO TURN TO, YOU WILL HOLD ON TO THE FIRST PERSON WHO SUPPORTS YOU

16) ZEYNEP LEAVES HER BEST FRIEND BEHIND... 1987

People didn't like Zeynep much because she would speak her mind like a 'square John' and would sometimes have an aggressive attitude. But if she loved or trusted a person, she would become extremely attached to that person. Although most people overlooked it, she actually had a very sensitive heart.

At the age of seventeen, her senior year in high school, she had a classmate named Doğa, who was one of those people. Doğa was a prescient and mature person, but her social skills were a bit weak. In contrast to Zeynep, who always claimed her rights, she was an introverted, quiet girl. One day, when a few children bothered her friend a lot and made her sad, Zeynep fiercely defended her and defeated all those children by herself. After that incident, Doğa became very attached to her.

Doğa's books were very important to her and she read whenever she could. She inherited her reading habit from her grandfather, who was a judge with a humanistic worldview. Since she had lost her father in a traffic accident at a young age, Doğa lived with her mother as well. Initially, she and her mother lived with her grandparents for a long time; both of which had been very helpful to their daughter and her baby.

Both friends had problems socializing, and they always supported each other in every way when they were together. Especially Zeynep told her about everything that made her angry, happy, or sad, opened up to her, and listened to her friend's suggestions. Doğa's remarks, who was a very mature girl, reminded Zeynep to look at things from different perspectives. Even though Zeynep didn't like what she said from time to time, deep down, she always believed that she was right, because she was rarely wrong. Her mother Füsun would give her some of the same information and advice that Doğa gave her. But Füsun would tell these things like a mother in a commanding, warning, and angry manner, but Doğa would tell them like a friend.

Unfortunately, they did not realize the class they entered in that June would be the last day of their happiness. It was Friday, the last day of the week, and they had just had their last class, and the weather was unbearably hot. The teacher had finished the lesson and told the students they were free to do what they wanted in the class. With the happiness of the beginning of the weekend, all the students were absorbed in their own world, and there was a low hum in the classroom. They were impatiently waiting for the freedom the school bell would bring, but it felt as if time stood still. They all had different thoughts and feelings, of course, but the only thing they had in common was that they were tired.

Even the student who knocked on the door and entered the classroom to say that the administration asked for the teacher did not change their slackness. After a while, the teacher came back to the classroom. "Children, listen to me for a minute," he said, standing in front of the board. Most of the students looked up at him. Then Zeynep saw the teacher and heard the words, which she would never forget and always remember whenever she thought of Doğa later in her life:

"Unfortunately, our friend Doğa Aslan will not be with us anymore. I just learned that they are moving to Bursa." Zeynep couldn't comprehend what she was hearing, and her first thought was 'Doğa would have told me if that was true'. Then she turned her head and looked at Doğa sitting next to her. Doğa leaned towards Zeynep quietly, and said,

"I know you should have heard it from me, but I just couldn't tell you." When she saw Zeynep looking at her with anger, she added,

"Please forgive me."

So her best friend, with whom she dreamed of going to university together after high school, was leaving. There was a brief chatter in the classroom; a few students asked questions to Doğa to get more detail from her. Some of the students returned to their own world after satisfying their curiosity and making their comments.

Zeynep was stuck in her seat and could not move for a long time. As Doğa touched her arm to say something, she withdrew her arm with fury and looked into Doğa's eyes with anger. After a few seconds of staring at each other, Zeynep looked away, irritated. Doğa, who was very upset about this, left the classroom without saying anything, shedding silent tears after the bell rang. Zeynep could find the strength to get up long after the class was empty, slowly stood up, and headed home with pain in her heart.

The weekend went badly for both of them. When Zeynep tried to talk with her mother about her friend's leave, thereby sharing her sadness with her, her mother said,

"For goodness sake! Friends will come and go. You will have many more friends throughout your life!" underrating Zeynep's problem and closing the subject. It took a long time for Füsun to pull herself together after the breakup with İlker, so did not feel well either, she was trying to cope with her own mental problems.

Thankfully, Doğa and Zeynep made up in a short time and decided to spend their last days better.

They continued their friendship with sadness and anxiety.

One Saturday, Zeynep wanted to buy a souvenir for her friend and asked her mother to go to the market. Füsun, unaware of her daughter's experiences and feelings, refused by saying,

"I have a meeting today, we can't go to the market." This was their last week with Doğa, and Doğa was important to her, whom she loved deeply. But her mother was so immersed in her own world that she could not realize it.

The fact that her father had left them, that they had to move from the house they lived together before, that she had to leave her best friend who was moving to another city, and Füsun's endless grumbles placed too heavy a burden on Zeynep's shoulders for her age. These events, each of which was a trauma for a child of that age, and the coming years, would lead to more serious psychiatric diseases.

Separating from her friend, to whom she was obsessively attached, was another trauma for Zeynep, who had so many radical changes in her family and was so disappointed with them.

YOU UNDERSTAND THE VALUE OF SOME PEOPLE IF YOU FEEL THE FEAR OF LOSING THEM

17) ZEYNEP'S DEEP DESPERATION... 1987

Zeynep, who was ten years old when her parents divorced, never led a healthy mental life. From that age, Füsun took her to psychiatrists and they had to change many doctors. Zeynep either didn't like the medicines given by the doctor, saying that they had a bad effect on her, or that she didn't like the doctor's attitude, or the doctor directed her to someone else because of health reasons. Almost all of the physicians said something different, which exasperated both. In the beginning, she was diagnosed with childhood depression, and she had to use a lot of medicine with different names and various doses from time to time. Zeynep had a sensitive soul, the divorce of her parents had affected her a lot; the divorce traumatized her in a way that would affect her daily life.

Sometimes she would peacefully cooperate with the doctor, sometimes she would lose her grip and tried to live her life in a nervous and unhappy way. She liked to spend time at home, as she generally did not get along very well with her peers. Paintings and painters had a special place in her inner world. Strangely enough, Zeynep was always self-sufficient until the age of fourteen or fifteen, or so everyone thought.

The years passed in an unpleasant way both for Zeynep and for Füsun. They were always at loggerheads, and there was always a reason to fight: Zeynep was either going home at a late hour, saying something terrible to Füsun, or slapping Yiğit so hard that his nose bled, or neglecting her duties…

When Zeynep started going to a private teaching institution to prepare for the university exam; she suffered from a sleep disorder and loss of appetite. She found it hard to fall asleep, she was always tossing and turning in her bed. In the mornings, however, she was stuck, unable to get out of bed, as if an invisible force tied her hands and feet. She would force herself to get up and feel exhausted and weary at school. During the day, she would feel gloomy. She had no appetite and was extremely weak. During the times she spoke to Füsun, although rarely, she was pessimistic about her future and said things that revealed she felt suffocating anxiety:

'Why did she keep on living?', 'If she were her father, she would leave her mother too', 'She would not accommodate anyone', 'No one loved her, why would anyone love her?' etc.

Feelings such as sadness and anxiety that most people experience from time to time and often attribute to the hustle and bustle of daily life were actually hinting at the disease Zeynep would suffer from in the future. But Füsun, who thought that it was the stress of preparing for the university exam, did not hear Zeynep's reproaches and cries for help at that time.

Zeynep would do the thing that would deeply affect and scare the whole family during that period when she felt so depressed and desperate after everyone went to bed. She had argued with Füsun again; she had done something wrong, which according to her mother she should not have done. Füsun had vented her spleen because of a trivial issue. As she often did in their mother-daughter fights, Zeynep had left the room crying again, gone to her room, and slammed the door.

At that moment, they had an intense feeling of worthlessness and being redundant in this world. She had no reason to live; moreover, her best friend had gone and abandoned her. These thoughts passed through her mind at the speed of light by the time she reached her bed. She saw the medicines by her bed the moment she got into bed; medicines that were always there on the shelf. Without thinking, she started to take them, one after another, out of the box and the blister pack, and pop them into her mouth like candy. She chugged a glass of water as tears rolled down her cheeks intensely. She lay down on her bed, closed her eyes, and began to think about how unhappy she was. Suddenly, she realized that she missed her father and wanted to see him; but it was too late now, he could come to her grave. She took the fetal position with her knees drawn up to her stomach, and fell into deep thoughts, waiting to calm down. As she lost consciousness, her past flashed before her eyes like a filmstrip.

An hour had passed when Füsun, who thought that Zeynep must have calmed down, went to her room to talk and saw pills and pillboxes scattered on the ground. Zeynep was lying curled up in her bed. Was she asleep or was she unconscious? She approached her and called out her name, first shaking her shoulders, and when she didn't wake up, she started to slap her cheeks. She realized that Zeynep was not conscious. She thought of what she had to do in seconds. Her downstairs neighbor and doctor friend Elif and her husband could help. She went downstairs in a fury with her house slippers on and started to bang on their door. She tried to explain to Elif, who opened the door with fear, that Zeynep took a lot of pills and tried to commit suicide, with fear and panic. Elif's husband, who heard what Füsun told, said,

"I'll get dressed and be right there," and went into the bedroom. Elif and Füsun went upstairs. Füsun was standing in the doorway crying while Elif entered Zeynep's room and checked at her pulse and pupils. She came back to her senses with Elif's voice, saying,

"Come on Füsun, put something on, Ahmet will be here any minute now." As Füsun went to her bedroom and got changed, her daughter Zeynep's childhood and cheerful memories passed before her eyes, tears pouring down from her eyes. On the way to the hospital, she prayed to God and made vows to Him to spare her daughter's life.

At the hospital, they immediately pumped Zeynep's stomach, told her that she would be kept under observation for follow-up purposes, and she was admitted to the Intensive Care Unit. All they could do now was to wait. After calming down a bit in the waiting room, hoping for good news from the doctors, Füsun realized that she had to call Emin. She didn't know what to do, how to say it, but she had to do it somehow.

Füsun, after telling him what had happened as best as she could, faced a very harsh reaction; Emin presumed to question her motherhood. Füsun didn't know what to say, who already had questioned herself as she waited in the waiting room and felt more and more dejected and sorrowful. She felt that she didn't deserve any sentence that will upset her, any statement against her from Emin, and that everything in her life, especially her ex-husband, lost its importance. She didn't want to listen to him and his questions anymore, she handed the phone to Elif and returned to her inner world and sorrow.

Towards morning, when she got the news that Zeynep was

in stable condition and overcame the risk of death, but that she had to be under observation in the hospital for a while longer, she started to cry again, but this time they were tears of joy. While she was sitting in the waiting room of the hospital, Füsun made very important decisions about the future. Decisions that would mature her and make her think more positively...

After thinking calmly, Emin regretted what he had said and called Füsun the next day to apologize. As a physician, he also questioned this situation, he couldn't understand why his daughter would do such a thing. He had realized that Zeynep didn't sound well at all during their most recent phone calls and that she was evasive when he had asked questions. He realized that she was in a depressed mood. Unfortunately, this dreadful attempt proved it. Although this depressive state could be seen in every field of occupation, he had read somewhere that artists were more susceptible to it, and about 20 percent of people who suffered from depression attempted suicide. Though it frightened him to think that, he couldn't help but think of artists like Vincent Van Gogh, Virginia Woolf, Sylvia Plath, Jack London, and Ernest Hemingway. One felt the need to learn about the childhood of these artists, whose creativity was wonderful and whose fate was dark. Did they have symptoms when they were just a child, before that ominous moment when they destroyed themselves, did the seeds of his diseases were planted in that period... The chemical, behavioral, and inherited disorders were so intricately intertwined that in the situation that made the person this way, Emin felt only an overwhelming sense of helplessness.

Considering what she had been through, he could only guess why Zeynep had come to this point, and at that moment he could do nothing but be sad.

SOME BEGINNINGS ALWAYS START WITH HOPE

18) YİĞİT IS SENT TO PRIVATE STUDY CENTER… 1990

When Füsun and Emin got divorced, this unpredictable change in Füsun's life added to the problems she had at work, and she was left confused, not knowing what to do next. She was in a depressed mood for a long time because of all these experiences.

Yiğit, who was only three years old at the time and went to kindergarten when Füsun needed psychological support, could not get much support from his mother. He had struggled with the problems of all children at his age until he grew up. Needless to say, he had an unhappy childhood. When his uncle and aunt approached Füsun to help her, whose anger did not mitigate for a long time, she refused every time, saying,

"I don't want any help from them." Only Cem managed to be with them despite Füsun.

Füsun, who has no hope for the future Zeynep, with whom she was in constant conflict, wanted to be cautious with Yiğit; she had him enrolled in a private study center during high school. He would go to this center, which was close to school, after school hours, review the lessons he learned at school, ask questions about the things he did not understand, and do his homework there.

Also, Füsun's aim was to keep Yiğit away from conflicts with Zeynep, with whom he often has a conflict. She thought that Zeynep was negatively affecting her son, who was a sensitive child. But when she would realize that the biggest negative influence on him was not only Zeynep but also the wrong decisions she had made, it would be too late...

A PERSON WHO IS VALUED WILL FEEL SPECIAL

19) DİLA MEETS HALİL... 1990

Dila, who was 13 years old when her older sister went to İzmir to attend high school and moved in with her grandmother, was left alone in that huge house in Urla.

Even though she and her mother saw each other every evening, she always felt her sister's absence and often thought 'I wish she was with me'.

While physiological changes were taking place in her body, storms were also breaking in her inner world.

Her mother had begun to spend time with Derya, her childhood friend, who had come and settled in Urla at that time, and whom she had not seen for a long time. Especially when she first arrived, her mother was always with her friend, and she started to spend much less time at home with her daughter. Due to her excessive benevolence, Gül was running around to help her friend, neglecting her home and daughter. She would go to her after work to help her settle into her new home and guide her on where the materials she needed were sold.

Dila, on the other hand, had important problems at school and in her soul. She also needed urgent answers to questions in her mind. She was asking questions and getting answers whenever she had the chance, but what she really needed was substantial moral support. She had made several attempts to talk to her mother, but she was either about to leave the house, or talking to Emin about something important, or she was on a phone call or had something important to do at that moment.

One evening when her mother met her friend Derya and came home late, Dila witnessed a conversation between her mother and Uncle Emin; her mother was saying,

"Derya is not well again," with a sigh. She was sitting in the blue armchair across Emin, tired and weary.

"I still don't understand why she is with that man," said Uncle Emin, without looking up from the book he was reading.

"Oh, if only I knew," her mother replied. Looking at the worry on their faces, Dila understood that something was wrong. Aunt Derya would stay over some nights, and she would have long conversations with her mother during those nights. Dila would be sent to her room and asked to deal with something else. Dila didn't like being sent to her room like this.

Actually, Aunt Derya was a very cheerful, talkative, and good woman. Sometimes when she came over happily, she would bring a lot of gifts for Dila; she would ask her how she was and chat with her. But sometimes, she would have a worried, unhappy, ready-to-cry expression on her face or she would cry all the time.

One day, Aunt Derya came to their house with a swollen face and a black eye. Dila, who could not believe her eyes, was very afraid of what she saw, so she decided that she should get out of the way, and she escaped to her room. Some people were much worse off than she was, who needed help more than she did, and it would be better if her mother helped them. As far as she could understand, Aunt

Derya's husband was a bad person. 'Who did that to her?', 'Who could treat a person like this?' She was asking herself, even though she, unfortunately, knew that the answer was someone did that to her. The image of Aunt Derya's face and devastated state would be imprinted in her mind, and she would never forget that for the rest of her life.

It was at that time that Dila started to see Halil, who supported her. She fought with her classmate Özge right before leaving school over a trivial issue, and after school, she disappeared among the trees next to the school, sitting on a bench. Özge was the best and only friend of Dila, who was already incapable of making friends. Her face was red, she was wiping the tears from her eyes with her tiny hands, and sighing from time to time. When she saw a white tissue in front of her, she raised her head to look at the person holding it out and she saw Halil. He was looking at Dila with his smiling hazel eyes and handsome clean face. Dila smiled at him as she took the tissue he held out and wiped her tears. After Halil sat next to her and found out why she was crying, he said,

"Even though we face difficulties, we must not give up," in a wise tone. He said that the event she told was not worth crying about and added, "Do you know the story of the two frogs?".

When she replied "No," he started to tell the story. While Halil was telling the story, Dila stopped crying while paying attention to the story, and started to carefully listen to what Halil was telling:

"One day, two little frogs, who loved to leap, were leaping again when they accidentally fell into a big bucket filled with milk. One of the frogs shouted, 'Oh no!'. 'This bucket is too high. We can't jump out of here!' 'No, there must be a way out,' said the second frog. The first frog struggled for a while. It lost hope when it couldn't get out. It stopped trying. And soon drowned in milk." Dila reacted,

"Oh!" with surprise. Then she turned towards Halil with curious eyes and asked, "What happened then?". Halil continued to tell the story with a know-it-all attitude:

"The second frog still had hope. It struggled, struggled, struggled... And never gave up. It struggled to the limit of its strength. But eventually, its arms were out of strength. It could no longer move its arms.' Oh no!' it said. 'What am I going to do now?' At that moment, it noticed that a heap of butter had formed in the milk. 'Oh my God!' it rejoiced. 'While I was struggling, some of the milk turned into butter.' It jumped happily on the butter. It lifted its head and looked up. It said, 'Now it's very easy to jump out'. It was out of the bucket in one leap. It was very happy to get out of the bucket of milk as it was leaping to the lake." Looking away, Halil turned his face to Dila, who was listening to the story with interest.

"Here," he said.

"We can also make our own butter in the face of the problems we have, right?" he asked, laughing sarcastically. Dila, who was looking at him with wide eyes, nodded silently. After this story, Halil stood up.

"I have to go now, see you!" he said, heading for the exit.

When Dila asked, "Will you come again?" he replied, "Of course, I will come one day, wait for me!" and left.

Now the first thing Dila did after school was to go and look at the secluded bench. Sometimes she found Halil sitting on the bench waiting for her. She would be happy whenever she saw him, she immediately would go and sit next to him. They always found something to talk about. Teachers, friends, experiences, feelings... While Dila was talking, Halil was looking at her with smiling eyes and listening to what she was telling him. Dila liked his soft voice and the remarks he made about what she told him.

If Dila did not see Halil sitting on the bench in that secluded place, she would be disappointed and return home sulking with sadness. Halil had told Dila that he was studying engineering, but he currently couldn't go to school due to health problems and he had to take a break. The chats on the bench soon turned into walking together and going to a patisserie, with Halil saying, "Come, let me buy you hot chocolate." He had begun to touch Dila while speaking. In between words, he would tweak her on the cheek and stroke her head when she said something he liked. Dila found Halil handsome and when she was walking next to him, she liked how he put his hand on her shoulder when he was telling her about something. Being with someone whose behavior towards her gave the message 'you are valuable' made her feel pleasure for being admired and she felt honored. Halil was physically crossing the line, but Dila thought she knew him by now and trusted him, so his behavior did not seem abnormal to her.

On the days she went home late, she was finding excuses like 'the class ran late', 'I forgot my notebook at school, I went back to get it,' not knowing why she was lying to the housekeeper woman working at their house. A voice inside her was saying that it would not be right to say, 'We walked along the streets with Halil' because they could try to prevent her from spending time with him.

In this way, Dila continued to meet with Halil. Until a colleague told Gül,

"I saw Dila in Atatürk Neighborhood yesterday evening, she was with a young boy." That neighborhood was in opposite direction from Dila's school.

"Are you sure it was Dila?" Gül asked worriedly.

"Of course I'm sure. Because I asked her how she was and we had a little chat," her friend replied. Gül wondered, 'What could her daughter be doing there at that hour?', 'Who was with her?' That day had been hard for her with her head full of thoughts and questions.

She left work a little earlier in the evening and went to wait in front of the school before the last class ended. She was sitting in her car; she was thinking about how she would ask Dila about this and what her attitude should be towards her.

Finally, the bell rang, and soon the children began to get out of the school. When she saw Dila coming out of the garden gate of the school, she got out of her car and realized that just as she was about to call out, Dila was walking to the opposite side of the garden wall. She got out of her car and headed that way. She saw Dila disappearing through the weeping willows and lemon cypresses leaning towards the pavement and forming a passage. When she slowly approached and looked a little more carefully, she saw that Dila was sitting there with someone on an old unpainted bench with missing boards. She was fervently telling him about something, and the person sitting next to her was listening. It sounded like she was talking about her teacher. Leaning under the trees, Gül stood at a distance from them in silence and began to watch them. Dila was the first to notice her and jumped up,

"Hey! Mom!" she said in surprise. Halil also got up and looked at Gül with eyes full of fear, not knowing what to do. After staring in silence for a while, Gül said,

"What's your name?" staring at Halil.

"Halil," he said quietly.

"How old are you?" she said with a menacing voice.

"Nineteen," Halil replied.

"What are you doing with my daughter?" Gül asked angrily.

"Mom, she is my friend!" cried Dila. Gül was so angry that she didn't even hear her.

"Tell me your last name," she said, staring at Halil. Halil lowered his head like a criminal,

"Yavuzer," he said with a barely audible voice. Without taking her eyes off him, Gül shouted,

"Get out of here before I give call the police!". While Halil was quickly walking towards the exit, she added,

"I don't want to see you near my daughter again!". Dila started to cry. Tears were flowing down her cheeks as she asked her mother why she sent him away like that.

"He didn't do anything!" she said, crying. Gül, who watched Dila for a while without reacting, almost hissed, "We will talk at home Dila! Come on, let's go!" she said, pointing the exit with her finger...

The days that followed were turbulent. Dila was very angry with her mother for treating her friend in that way and would not stop making a scene at home at every opportunity. Gül also talked to the housekeeper woman working at their home and found out that Dila had been coming home late for about two months. She also had her fair share of Gül's anger for not informing her in time.

In Urla, where everyone knew each other because it was a small place, Gül asked around about Halil through her acquaintances at the police station; she learned that he had lost his father at a young age, he lived with his mother and had psychological problems. And that he had a world of his own, he dropped out of middle school and lived in a one-room house with his poor mother...

This incident involved the risk of becoming a major disaster and if not intervened, Dila could have been irreversibly affected mentally or physically. Thankfully, she had noticed it in time and intervened in this incident, which made her shudder whenever it came to her mind. She did not tell Alper about this incident, which she had trouble explaining even to herself and bothered her for many years. She would not be able to give a satisfactory explanation even if she told him about it. At such a time, when this crisis was averted, Gül questioned her motherhood, and Dila did not want to go to school or even think about not going out of the house, the phone call they received from Alper would completely change the direction of their lives...

THE MORE HOPEFUL YOU ARE, THE MORE DISAPPOINTED YOU WILL BE WHEN THINGS GO WRONG

20) ALYA STARTS UNIVERSITY IN ISTANBUL AND MEETS CEM... 1990

When Alya finished high school and got accepted into the Faculty of Law of Istanbul University, Cem was in his fourth year at Cerrahpaşa Faculty of Medicine. Emin called his son Cem and asked him to help Alya, who was in Istanbul for enrollment in the university. For the sake of his father and Aunt Gül, who always treated him well during the summers he had spent in Urla, Cem called her. He hadn't seen Alya in years at that point and he was reluctant to call her.

Alya was surprised when the landlady, who said she could use her phone for emergencies, knocked on the door to say that there was someone on the phone who wanted to talk to her. She would have a phone line connected to her house later, but at that time, she was calling her parents from the payphone when necessary. Worried about this unexpected phone call, Alya quickly went to her landlady's house.

She was surprised to hear Cem's voice, who introduced himself as "Hello, I'm Cem Başar." There was a formal exchange in which they inquired after each other's health. Then, Cem said that he wanted to see her, that there might be things she might want to know about Istanbul, and that he would be happy to help her. They agreed to meet the next day under the Galata Tower, the place Alya knew the best.

It was a beautiful and sunny day in October. Alya was waiting at the café where they agreed to meet. When she looked up from the magazine in her hand, she saw and recognized Cem, who was coming from across the café. When she raised her hand for him to see her, Cem recognized her too and headed to her table with a smile. Alya felt a sense of excitement when she thought of the summers they had spent together in the same house as little children. It was amazing how time has flown by. Cem looked very handsome in his light blue T-shirt and navy blue jeans. Alya thought he looked a lot like his father with his blonde hair and blue eyes, that he was even a bit more handsome than his father. They both seemed content as they ordered their drinks after a short exchange of asking each other if they were well.

During the time they spent at the café, they reminisced about the past, made fun of their parents, talked about their siblings, and about what they had been doing during the years until starting university there. They talked about a lot of things and lost track of time. Both of them were having such a good time that Cem, who had thought that he would leave after ten minutes, was still freely talking about things nonstop, making Alya laugh with his jokes even after hours had passed.

When they got together during summers in the past, although not often, they would usually only see each other during dinnertimes. They had very different interests from each other. Cem would set up his own group of friends, usually going out with them after dinner and arriving home late at night. Cem had visited them in Urla for only a few summers as a child, and as he grew older, his visits became even rarer.

When Alya returned home in the evening, she was unable to contain herself, she felt as if she was flying over the clouds. What a beautiful day she had. They had spent hours at that café. She liked Cem very much. She was sure he liked her too. She applied to many universities in various cities, especially Izmir, but she was at one in Istanbul. According to her, this meant that her life would intersect with Cem's life, and they would be together. It was in the nature of youth to hope for something and believe that it would come true. The energy expended to achieve this wouldn't mean anything. But Alya didn't know yet facing the truth in the future would feel like having a tiger by the tail. She didn't know that it would hurt her for a long time, and how helpless she would be in quenching this inflammation.

They kept seeing each other in this way for several months. Alya adapted to the university immediately; she was going to her classes with great enthusiasm. She was impressed by Cem and was looking forward to the days when she would see him again, trying to create opportunities to meet him. She went to the faculty where Cem studied to see him several times, and Cem had come to hers to see her. They had long chats, enjoying their time together each time. They met outside a few times too, had a drink, and went to the movies. Cem's close friend Emre joined them once, but Alya didn't like Emre, who spoke a lot and tried to make jokes at every opportunity. Of course, Alya did not know at that time that her path would somehow cross with Emre in the future and that she would never like it.

But after a while, whenever Alya called to meet, Cem had an excuse such as he has a shift, he had an exam, he had a basketball game, and even though he knew Alya now had a phone line at her house, he didn't call her. Although Cem, who played in the basketball team of the faculty, told her that he may not have time because of the training and courses, Alya was getting increasingly worried about why he did not call her. She would probably get even more worried, until one day she would receive a phone call from Cem.

After asking how she was and a little chat, Cem invited Alya to a tea party in four days held by a university committee, of which he was a member. When Cem said,

"I would love it if you could come to this party," there was a brief silence on the other end of the phone. Alya could not believe her ears; she could not speak for a while. When Cem asked,

"Alya are you there?" she responded,

"Yes, I'm here," with a happy voice.

"Where will the party be?" she asked excitedly. After describing the place where the party will be held, Cem apologized, reminding her that he was on the organizing committee, and said,

"Unfortunately, you will have to come by yourself, dear Alya, I won't be able to pick you up," jokingly. Alya said, "Oh! Yes, of course, I can come by myself," she replied.

Alya excitedly went shopping the next day after her classes. She needed to buy some new things, she had to look beautiful. She had to go to a lot of stores around Istanbul; she needed a dress and matching jewelry, shoes, and a matching purse. When she was finally convinced that she had bought the right things and finished shopping, it was late in the evening, and Alya returned home exhausted. Despite being so tired, her overflowing happiness did not slow her down, and she danced to the upbeat music playing on her radio the rest of the night. The thought of seeing Cem swept her off her feet until the day of the party, making her feel like she was flying above the clouds.

Four days later, Alya arrived at the place where the tea party would be held and got out of the taxi. As she entered the room, she looked stunning in a dark green chiffon dress that ended just above her ankle, with a cleavage, emphasizing her green eyes even more. And there were sparkles in her auburn hair, which was pinned up high to reveal her long neck.

As she entered the ballroom through the door adorned with white lilies and looked around, people were turning their heads to look at her, to this person they didn't know, with curious eyes. Alya, who looked beautiful enough to attract attention, saw Cem sitting at a crowded table. While walking towards him, Cem saw her too, got up from the table right away, and went towards her.

"Alya, You look great," he said, kissing her on the cheeks. After this move, which excited Alya very much, he took her hand and said,

"Come," taking her to the table where he was sitting and introduced her to his friends one by one.

"My step-sister Alya; she just started law school," he said when introducing her. For some reason, Alya didn't like the word 'sister' that Cem used. The people at the table said 'nice to meet you', looking at her with admiration. They couldn't take their eyes off Alya. Cem, who showed Alya a seat at the table, said,

"Excuse me," and left. When Alya was left alone with Emre, who was sitting next to her and whom she had met before and didn't like very much, she thought that Cem would come back immediately. Emre, who immediately started chatting with her, was very happy to see Alya. He kept talking nonstop to keep her attention on himself; the conversation was more like a monologue rather than a dialogue. On the one hand, Alya was looking for Cem with her eyes around the room, and on the other hand, she was answering Emre's questions with a forced smile on her face.

When Emre asked her to dance, Alya could not refuse and had to get up to dance. During the dance, Emre said,

"You look so beautiful," Alya replied briefly,

"Thanks." Emre continued,

"Do you even realize that you are the prettiest girl at the party?". Alya thought that Emre would not stop and continue to talk like this, which made her afraid. She wasn't sure she wanted to hear what he had to say. Don't say anything more, please, she thought.

While dancing, she saw Cem from afar. He was not alone, there was a beautiful girl next to him and his hand was on her shoulder. They came to the table where Alya was sitting earlier while hugging each other; they stood there and started to have a cheerful conversation with a small group sitting there.

Alya, who was still dancing with Emre on the dance floor, could not take her eyes off them. When the dance song ended, they took their seats, and she overheard Cem telling someone at the table,

"Pelin has just arrived, she had a small problem with her key," she realized that what she had always feared had happened. When Cem approached her to introduce Pelin, she couldn't get up from her seat, she was petrified with disappointment. Cem was saying something, but Alya did not hear any of it because there was a buzzing in her ears.

She heard the words "Pelin studies English Language and Literature at Istanbul University," but her brain could not process them and turn them into meaningful sentences. Alya's head was starting to spin, but she was still trying to smile. Cem had his arm around Pelin's shoulder. Pelin was holding Cem's hand hanging down from her shoulder, and taking it to her cheek from time to time. You would have to be a fool not to understand the attraction between them while seeing them looking into each other's eyes while talking, leaning onto each other while laughing, Pelin's reaching out and stroking Cem's hair. Alya vaguely remembered extending her hand and saying,

"Nice to meet you." Cem was probably saying something about her, but the loud music and the buzzing in her ears prevented her from understanding what he was saying. When she calmed down a bit, Alya had the opportunity to scrutinize Pelin.

Pelin was a very beautiful and charming person, she had long blond hair and blue eyes. She wore a black dress that showed off her slim body. It was obvious that she loved Cem very much. She would later find out that she was very ambitious and a go-getter. When Cem and Pelin walked away from their table, only Emre remained next to her, who was still talking. She did not hear at all what he was saying, nor did she want to hear; all she wanted right now was for him to shut up and leave her alone with the pain of being there at that moment.

At a moment when Pelin and Cem were not in sight, Alya realized that she could not stand to be there any longer; despite Emre's insistence for her to stay, she left after a short while saying she had a headache. She was only able to say.

HAVING AN ARTISTIC PERSONALITY OPENS UP DIFFERENT PERSPECTIVES ON LIFE

21) ZEYNEP'S FIRST LOVE SİNAN... 1991

As children become adults, they form a personality with multifactorial effects such as how they perceive the world, their social environment, and the character traits in their genes. One of the three children of the "Başar Family," in which the parents were divorced, Zeynep had a difficult adolescence period. Füsun raised her children by putting pressure on them, admonishing them, interfering with their privacy, which she thought was her right, but also backfired, causing conflicts between her and Zeynep. Zeynep was shutting herself in her room in the evenings, sometimes without saying a word, in order not to see her mother, with whom she was never on good terms.

When she wanted to be alone, she did what she enjoyed the most since she was a little child: painting. For this reason, Zeynep decided to study what she loved the most and got into the painting department of Adana Fine Arts Academy. She decided to study in that department one year after graduating from high school.

She realized that she had made the right decision when the classes started. She found herself a nice group of friends, and on top of that, she had a boyfriend.

Her therapy was also going well with her psychiatrist, whom she had been seeing since the age of ten. She was using her medications regularly and was getting the maximum benefit from psychotherapies. Füsun was also supporting her, doing her best to solve their problems with the least damage. During adolescence, most of their mother-daughter conflicts had decreased to almost none. As Füsun questioned herself retrospectively, she realized her mistakes and decided to be more relaxed; she was also getting more mature along with her daughter and son.

Zeynep was about to finish her first year of university when she met Sinan. Sinan had graduated from Ankara University Faculty of Political Sciences and worked at a local newspaper. He was a handsome man who liked to talk, had a wide social circle, and liked to have fun and enjoy the blessings of the world. According to Zeynep, who preferred to be by herself, he was very successful in meeting new people and maintaining relationships. Zeynep was twenty-one and Sinan was twenty-five when they started dating shortly after one of Sinan's friends from university introduced them. Sinan had always been interested in colorful and wild people he thought enlivened his life, so he was very interested in Zeynep, who was a very unique person herself.

Sinan enjoyed writing very much. He had a column in Yeni Adana Newspaper, where he was working at that time, and wrote on various subjects. His eyes sparkled when enthusiastically sharing what he wrote with Zeynep or someone else, and no one could stop him when he started to talk about writing, books, and authors. The writing was his way of life, and he always had hoped to become a well-known author in the future. He would feel on top of the world whenever his stories or poems were published in a newspaper or magazine.

After getting to know him, Zeynep's life also gained meaning with him. It was the first time she had met someone who valued her so much. Zeynep, whom Sinan sometimes called "Zeynom" and sometimes "my soul mate," trusted him no end. Zeynep shared everything about her life with him, her father leaving them, her conflicts with her mother, her siblings, her step-siblings, her suicide attempt.

When Sinan had no work in the city, he would get in his car and come to the university; he liked to spend his time in the school cafeteria of the faculty – even in the cafeterias of other faculties. He acquired a wider circle of friends – including instructors – there than Zeynep did. It was sufficient for Sinan to overhear a student sharing a problem with friends. If there was anything he could do to help that person, he would do everything he could. Because his circle was so wide, he knew just the right person to call in that situation and would call that person immediately. He helped many people and solved problems for many students who were just out of high school. They loved Sinan, whom they called 'brother-in-law', at least as much as they loved Zeynep – some even more so than Zeynep, Zeynep would always say.

ONE MIGHT SUBSTITUTE SOMEONE FOR AN ABSENT PARENT

22) YİĞİT MEETS MUSTAFA... 1992

On a Monday with a warm spring wind, Yiğit was sitting on the bench under a tree in front of the study center, eating his sandwich without appetite. In this place where he came and sat after leaving school, he was waiting for his class, which would start in a little while. He was tearing pieces from the bread of his sandwich and throwing them at the cat in front of him, which was looking into his eyes as if asking for food. After eating the bread Yiğit gave it, the cat lifted its head as if asking for more. Yiğit, who was immersed in his own world, occupied with the cat, was silently sitting next to Mustafa on the bench.

He came to his senses when he heard the words "That cat belongs here, this is its home." Yiğit replied,

"Yeah, I've been seeing it for some time."

"It is very sweet, its name is 'Hunter'," said Mustafa.

"Hunter," repeated Yiğit and said,

"Nice name," with a smile. Yiğit was looking at the cat, and Mustafa was looking at Yiğit.

"What grade are you in?" Mustafa asked.

"I'm in the tenth grade," replied Yiğit. They met when Mustafa said,

"I'm Mustafa," and extended his hand. Later, their friendship continued with Mustafa's questions, who was trying to have conversations with Yiğit. Yiğit was amused by Mustafa's witty remarks, his making fun of the teachers, and his know-it-all attitude.

Yiğit continued to attend the study center with his mother's insistence and forcefully entered the classes, was talking to Mustafa reluctantly at first. When the conversation got longer and he glanced at his watch, he realized with amazement how quickly time had passed and he had missed the class. He jumped to his feet, wanting to catch the second class, saying

"See you later, I have to go to class," as he ran towards the study center building.

Later on, they often saw each other at the study center. When they see each other, Mustafa would raise his hand, saying,

"High five!" and would pull him towards himself by his hand when Yiğit would raise his hand for a high five, friendly patting him on the back with his other hand. He would ask if he needed anything with a brotherly attitude; Yiğit was feeling happy whenever he saw him.

One day, Yiğit got out of the study center exhausted and was waiting for the minibus. As he was about to step into the minibus at the bus stop, he started to quarrel with a group of kids who stood in front of him intending to tease him. But then the argument escalated and got physical, which lead to swearing and punching.

After the minibus left, the children started walking towards Yiğit. They started to push him on his shoulders. Mustafa was passing by, he saw the situation and came running to help him. He raised his voice and said,

"What are you doing, huh?" scaring the kids, kicking and swearing at them, making them go away. Then he approached Yiğit, put his hand on his shoulder, and asked

"Are you okay bro?" Of course, Yiğit thought Mustafa was helping him, he did not even think that this event was staged by Mustafa and his friends to make Yiğit grateful to him. During that academic year, Yiğit and Mustafa's friendship got deeper and they started to meet more often. At every opportunity, Mustafa would tell Yiğit, who was preparing for the university entrance exam, "I couldn't pass the exam because unfortunate events happened to me in the previous years, but this year I will pass it for sure."

Yiğit was unaware that Mustafa, who was twenty years old, stopped by the study center from time to time and was not regularly attending the classes. As far as he could see, Mustafa was a person liked by everyone; in addition, he was very brave. He supported Yiğit in all issues, took care of him like an elder brother, and listened to him with attention, so Yiğit had a lot of trust and admiration for him.

One day when they had the opportunity to chat for a long time, Mustafa told Yiğit about his sad life story. In this story that deeply affected Yiğit, he recounted how his beloved brother died; he told about how he had been unable to save him while he was dying, despite all his efforts. Moreover, despite all the sacrifices he had made, his ungrateful family eventually ostracized him.

"You look a lot like my deceased brother. So you're my brother now," he said at the end of his story. Later, he started to call Yiğit "my brother."

Yiğit trusted Mustafa, who never had a brother in his life, so much that he believed these stories without question, his exaggerated stories that were mostly imaginary.

INNER PEACE MAKE PEOPLE HAPPY

23) DİLA IS WITH SEVİNÇ IN ADANA... 1991

Dila, who was still angry at her mother for preventing her from seeing Halil and whose famous stubbornness had peaked, was over the moon when her father said on the phone,

"How would you like to go to high school in Adana?". She loved Adana, his father, and Sevinç. Her mother was with Emin in Urla, and Alya was in Izmir, which was a forty-five-minute drive away. Her father also had the right to be with someone from his own family, and that person could very well be Dila. She had wanted to live with her father for a long time, she was imploring her mother for it. Despite that, she was being rejected every year.

This proposal of her father, which caused a small crisis at home, increased the conflicts in their mother-daughter relationship, which was already tense. The efforts of Gül, who had to have dozens of conversations with Alper over the phone, were of no use in the end. Finally, it was decided that Dila would move to Adana.

The fact that Dila would move in with them also made Sevinç, his father's wife, very happy. At first, she thought that Gül would convince her not to live in Adana, but she was very happy when she heard that she was not successful. One day after it was decided that Dila would move in with them, Sevinç's mother, who was busy preparing food in the kitchen, said,

"Are you sure you want to live with Alper's daughter? Have you thought about it thoroughly?".

"Yes mom, I thought about it," Sevinç replied. Religion had a very important place in Sevinç's life, who welcomed her husband's daughter in her home, saying,

"I will both be a mother to Dila, and I will have done a good deed by saving her from her stepfather's house." Her mother said,

"Such kids of divorced parents are usually problematic, you might have to deal with that too."

"Mom, I know Dila, she is not like that at all, she is a quiet and easy-going child," she replied.

"What does her mother say about this? How will she send her daughter to live in her stepmother's house? I'm amazed!" said the woman, widening her eyes.

"There is no problem with that, mom," said Sevinç.

Her mother returned to her work in the kitchen, grumbling, "The person who has little faith has little love too."

"Don't say that, mom!" Sevinç looked at her angrily.

"Suit yourself, I just don't want your marriage to be damaged!" her mother added.

IF YOU LOVE SOMEONE, YOUR HOPE OF CHANGING THINGS WILL NEVER END

24) ALYA AND CEM ARE TOGETHER AGAIN AFTER MONTHS... 1991

After the school ball that ended badly, which she practically escaped from, Alya retreated into her shell and continued to live there. She continued her studies with a calm, excitement-free life of her own choice. She didn't see a lot of people, and she always had an excuse to refuse her friends' requests to meet. When she thought over what happened when she was alone in the evenings, she realized that both she and Cem had made mistakes, but only she was blinded by love. Yes, a voice inside her screamed that Cem might have a girlfriend, but she shut her ears to that voice; she didn't want to hear it, ignoring the fact that something like this could happen. Cem had also been very successful in not showing it, even through implication. Even though she was angry with him for this, her love was overriding all other feelings.

After that infamous ball, although Alya and Cem did not

see each other for a long time, Emre called her several times to meet. Each time, Alya refused for different reasons. One Friday evening after a long break, Cem called again, talked to her on the phone as if nothing had happened, made jokes, and Alya listened to him through heartaches. Insisting that she should meet Emre, Pelin, and him to spend time with them tomorrow, Cem did not leave anything to say to Alya. After some insistence, he finally convinced her. 'Why do I still have hope?' Alya bitterly asked herself, I always want to hear his voice, listen to his words, see his blue eyes,' but could not find the answer.

The next day was Saturday and the four of them were going to meet on Istiklal Street. While they were talking on the phone, Alya felt that she missed Cem immensely and that she wanted to see him. She especially missed his smile. It wasn't that she wasn't wondering about Pelin either; there had been little opportunity to speak to her that night. She was a very beautiful girl, yes, but her personality was important too. There were crazy questions in her mind, to which she was dying to find out the answers, such as 'What is she like?', 'Is she worthy of Cem?', 'Does she love him?', 'I wonder if they are happy?'... What would the answers do for her, what would she prove to herself, this was one of the questions she was asking herself as well.

The next day, on a bleak Saturday afternoon with no sunshine, the four of them got together. They met at the Tramvay Café on Istiklal Street as agreed. They enjoyed having food and drink with the excitement and happiness of youth.

Emre, who was overjoyed, showed much interest in Alya. He was looking her in the eye, doing his best to include her in the conversation, to make her laugh. Pelin liked Alya; she was asking her questions about her family and Izmir. Emre, too, was attentively listening to Alya's answers and showing his appreciation with his words.

With a smile on his face, Cem watched his two friends having fun, shaking his head from side to side, joining the conversation from time to time. Alya spoke very little as well. Today, the main actors of the conversation were Pelin and Emre. Cem was silent and looked sad; Alya wondered why. While watching him during the conversations, she felt that her heart was on fire, and she felt like reaching out and kissing him.

While the conversation in the café continued like this, Alya was busy struggling with thoughts like 'whatever I do, it's no use.' She felt redundant there, which hurt her. After having their meals and leaving the café, Emre suggested a walk towards Taksim.

Alya, who was overwhelmed indoors and thought that walking in that weather would be good to relieve her distress a little, took a deep breath when she stepped outside even though it got a little darker and colder outside. Besides, once they were outside, it would be easier to leave them to get on a minibus and go home.

They started walking slowly while talking at the same time. After walking for a while, Cem and Pelin stopped to look at a store window.

After getting away from them a little, Emre started to tell her that he liked her a lot, that he wanted to be with her forever, that his intentions were very serious, and that if she accepted his offer, everything would be great. As Emre continued his speech with a pleading face, Alya realized that this meeting was a setup arranged by the three of them. This meeting was designed just so that Emre could open up to her and Cem was also involved in this. Alya staggered again with disappointment and frustration. Again, all she wanted was to leave and to cry out loud… She told Emre that such a thing would not be possible at the expense of hurting him and that she did not share his feelings. She could not stay there any longer after this speech, and left after saying,

"Good evening," before they had a chance to ask her anything.

"Oh my God, what happened, where did Alya go all of a sudden," said Pelin, looking behind her. Meanwhile, the rain had begun to drizzle like Alya's tears. With her hands in the pockets of her coat and her eyes on the ground, she thought, "He is not mine, and he never will be," as she quickly walked towards the bus stop; her thoughts were getting mixed up, becoming more inextricable.

She resented herself for a long time for not taking a lesson from her experiences. Again, she built a wall around herself to heal her wounds, isolated herself from the world and settled down to her classes. She forgot Cem and her problems as she lost herself in those big law books weighing tens of kilos with hundreds and hundreds of pages and different colored covers.

One evening, she was startled by the phone ringing while she was watching TV. It was almost ten o'clock. When she picked up the receiver, thinking who could be calling at this hour, she heard Cem's voice, saying,

"I thought you would never answer the phone." Her heart started beating very fast again.

She couldn't speak for a few seconds.

"Hello? Are you there, Alya?" Cem's voice brought her to herself.

"Yes, I'm here, Cem," said Alya. After asking her how she was, Cem said,

"Do you know that Emre is not well?".

"Why? I hope nothing's wrong," Alya asked curiously and naively.

"He got depressed because you rejected him," replied Cem.

Alya didn't know what to say. These things could not be forced.

"He asked me to find out why you turned down his requests to meet," said Cem.

"Do I have to go somewhere with him? Do I have to go out with him?" she asked, her voice getting louder. Now it was Cem who was quiet. After a long silence, he said,

"You're right, of course, you don't have to."

"I don't want you to keep asking, Emre on the one hand and you on the other. I don't have to explain why I don't want to meet him, especially to you," she said. She was so angry that her patience had run out.

She felt angry and in a lot of pain; now there he was, asking her 'Why don't you go out with Emre?'.

"I'm sorry, I think I pushed you too hard," said Cem this time. There was a short silence on both ends of the phone again.

"You don't need to apologize," she said sternly.

"Cem, I want to hang up the phone; take care of yourself" she added and hung up the phone. She knew she shouldn't see him anymore. She had learned many lessons from her experiences.

Alya, who could not understand what Cem was trying to do, suffered for days and lost sleep for many nights. After long struggles and fights with her own heart, she decided not to see Cem again. She turned down all of Cem's requests to meet. She was very cold towards Cem when he came to her campus to see her, and refused his request to sit down and have a drink, making excuses. Alya, who buried her love and her pain in her heart, would believe that Cem and these experiences had an effect on being lost in her books, becoming a successful student always ranking high in her classes, and later becoming a successful lawyer, and she would always be grateful to him.

Alya would never find what she was looking for despite her attempts at dating several people, and she would never get married. After hearing from her mother that Cem got married, she would cry a lot as the memories would flash before her eyes like a film strip. She would never forget him, but they would meet for the first time in a long time because of the disaster that would bring the whole family together years later.

CHILDHOOD FRIENDSHIPS ARE ALWAYS STRONG

25) DILA STARTS SCHOOL IN ADANA... 1991

Children's summer meetings in Urla had continued for many years, and their relationships had developed in different ways over the years according to their personalities and expectations.

When Emin and Gül got married, Dila, the youngest of the children, was unaware of most things, and Yiğit, who was quiet like her, had always been on good terms. They were the same age and they got used to each other from an early age. When Dila came to Adana to move in with her father and go to high school, they had her enrolled in the private Gündoğdu College, which Yiğit had been attending since middle school. They were not in the same class, but they would see each other during breaktimes, sometimes they would smile at each other, sometimes they would talk. The two step-siblings, whose classes were in the same building, always felt each other's presence, never stopped supporting or loving each other.

In one of Dila's clearest childhood memories as an adult, Yiğit was saving Dila from two girls who were trying to lock her in her locker on the school hallway; he had taken one by her ponytail and the other by the collar of her shirt, taking them away from Dila, shouting,

"Leave her alone!". The girls had run down the corridor, staggering backward and crying. Yiğit had hurt them and frightened them. Dila had looked at him gratefully and in a barely audible voice,

"Thank you," she had said. When Sevinç put pastries and cookies in Dila's lunchbox, her eyes would look for Yiğit during breaks to share them with him. His silence, calmness, and the sadness in his eyes impressed the soft-hearted Dila very much, she felt a love for him with pity and an instinct of protecting him. Yiğit, who did not get along with Zeynep at home, was affected by his mother's unhappiness and missed his brother and father, he was doing everything off his own bat and his sensitive soul was increasingly withdrawing into himself.

Their high school years were spent watching and helping each other in this way, but towards the end of high school, Dila began to feel that things were not going well in Yiğit's life. She had asked him several times, but every time Yiğit would say,

"There's nothing to worry about," or

"Everything is fine," not telling her anything.

In the last days of high school, Yiğit began to come to school less often and on the days he did come, he did not look good, which did not escape Dila's attention, and this situation made her uneasy. Every time she saw him, Yiğit always looked tired, sleepless, and overly nervous...

FRIENDSHIPS ARE SHAKEN WHEN THERE IS JEALOUSY

26) CEM'S FEELINGS TOWARDS ALYA...

Cem was having a busy week due to an intercollegiate basketball tournament that week and he was tired, so when he heard his phone ringing, which ruined his plan to sleep late on the weekend, he swore out. With sleepy eyes, he grumbled,

"Who is this in the early morning?" walking to the phone in the living room. It was his father who was calling, and he was saying that his step-daughter Alya was in Istanbul, that she got into law school; he was asking him to find her and help her. Cem, holding his anger inside for his father, who woke him up that early in the morning -it was ten o'clock- said,

"Would she want such a thing?" trying to resist in his own way. His father replied,

"You give it a try, if she doesn't want to, she'll show it somehow. You will act accordingly," counterattacking his resistance.

Cem said, "Okay, dad," and hung up the phone. He vaguely remembered her as the chubby Alya, whose eyes were hidden behind wide bone-rimmed glasses, who spoke little and kept her head down. They had not met for years.

Zeynep would talk about her from time to time; her remarks were sometimes positive but sometimes they were full of disappointment, depending on her current mood.

In the afternoon, he called Alya from the fixed phone number that belonged to Alya's landlady, given by his father. When he introduced himself, Alya was very surprised and she answered warmly. She accepted Cem's offer to meet and they agreed to meet after school tomorrow.

The next day, as Cem was walking towards the place where they agreed to meet, he was thinking, 'I'll sit down for ten minutes, ask her if she needs anything, then find an excuse and leave'. He had more important things to do; was he supposed to waste his time with her? What a task his father had given him...

As Cem unwillingly entered the café - moreover, he was late - where he was going to meet Alya as per his father's request and looked around, he was thinking, 'How am I supposed to recognize her'. He caught sight of a beautiful girl who was looking at him intently with a smile. When the same girl raised her hand to be noticed, Cem could not believe his eyes. In front of him was a beautiful girl in a pink t-shirt, navy blue jeans, and long shiny hair in a ponytail. That girl had nothing to do with the Alya he knew from the past. He couldn't take his eyes off her as he walked towards the table, he was smiling happily and was thinking, 'Her eyes are green, I hadn't noticed that before'.

It was a beautiful October day, they were sitting under a tree in the garden of the café; as time passed by, they warmed to each other and the conversation got deeper. Although it was their first meeting, they did not realize how the time had passed.

As they started to meet more frequently, he felt excited when he was with Alya and realized that his feelings were evolving into things he never wanted. Yes, Cem was impressed by Alya a lot, but he was always afraid to admit it even to himself.

For that reason, Cem started to refuse to meet Alya after a while every time she called, finding excuses such as his exams, shifts, basketball games. Although he knew that she had a phone line connected to her house, he gave up on calling her after picking up the receiver and dialing her number halfway. Because he owed loyalty to Pelin. Pelin had been with him for years, during his exam times, she did his grocery shopping, prepared him meals, paid the electricity and water bills of the house, and did her best to make sure that Cem could concentrate on his exams. Besides, she was madly in love with him. For that reason, he couldn't become close with Alya, he couldn't let loose his feelings towards her. He had to stay away from her. He could not leave Pelin, who had stuck with him for years, one year before graduation.

He remembered the ball he helped organize. He remembered that night when Alya walked through the door of the ballroom in her green dress, and how all heads turned her way. As she walked towards him, he got up from his seat, greeted her, and couldn't help his heart racing as he placed a kiss on her cheek. As he took her by the hand and led her to the table where he was sitting, he felt that he was out of breath, and unfortunately, he realized that his feelings for her were not to be underestimated.

He said "excuse me" and left, doing everything not to be around her during the ball. Because Cem was afraid, he was afraid that he might act weakly, that irretrievable words would come out of his mouth. Later, while looking at Alya from afar, he saw her dancing with Emre. Seeing them like that, realizing that the emotion he felt was jealousy, his fear grew bigger. He had run away from the environment and from Alya to avoid the admiring glances of his friends towards her.

While introducing her to Pelin, it was as if he had seen Alya's confused face and felt her disappointment. Even though it wasn't real, he had done his best to paint the picture of a 'happy couple in love' in front of Alya. The next day, with a shattered heart, he felt the need to call Alya and ask her where she had suddenly gone at night, and he waited for the answer with pain in his heart...

Emre tried to tell him he wanted to call Alya and see her several times with various excuses, but he always received negative answers. But his insistence would go on. He yearned to see her, believing that sooner or later he would break Alya's stubbornness. That day, too, he nagged Cem to convince Alya to meet and to do something about it.

Although Cem did not take kindly to this, he could not stand Emre's insistence and reluctantly called Alya. He would insist that the four of them meet, and he would later feel guilty for doing so.

The day before they met, Emre talked about his treacherous plan while they were sitting at the school cafeteria during lunch break. He wanted him and Pelin to leave them so that he could open up to Alya the next day.

Cem had to say "Okay," getting angry with Emre who used him for such a thing.

The weather was good during that time, it was when fall was just starting to show its face in Istanbul when it suddenly got worse and started raining. With the end of the summer, sadness was felt more intensely, especially in young people, and emotional changes were experienced more frequently.

On the day they met, the weather was dark and unpleasant like Cem's inner world. Seeing Alya after a long time, realizing that he missed her caused heartache. He did not respond to Pelin and Emre's efforts for conversation; he didn't feel like it. He realized that Alya seemed unhappy as well.

On that phone call he made because of Emre's insistence, who was still hopeful and did not yield despite being refused by Alya on the day they met, Cem had said,

"Why don't you meet Emre? He got depressed because you rejected him!". Cem, who was scolded by Alya for these words, would never forget that phone call and the embarrassment he felt for the rest of his life.

When she said "I want to hang up the phone" and hung up, Cem was stunned. He thought that he made her very angry, that he deserved the scolding he got, and he was very upset. He had asked himself many times why he did stupid things because of Emre. His answer was, if Alya and Emre ended up together, he would have to give up on her too.

He realized that Alya also had feelings for him, and he was willing to sacrifice his and Alya's feelings because of the vow he made to himself that he would never make Pelin go through the same things his father made his mother go through. Since he was not willing to let her suffer as well, he thought the solution was to stay away from Alya.

And this incident with Emre added to his sadness and shook him.

They were in a period when the semester was about to end, had a lot of exams and shifts, which made Cem and Emre tired. They would soon graduate as new physicians. They started to meet infrequently, as their internships were different and they were very busy. Emre, who lived with his family and used to invite Cem to dinner frequently, had not even called him for a long time. He was trying to stay away from Cem as much as possible, avoiding even eye contact, and immediately leaving the room he entered. Cem tried to talk several times, but Emre refused each time, saying,

"I'm busy right now." Cem could not make sense of Emre's

behavior and was looking for an opportunity to talk to him. He finally got that opportunity in the cafeteria he entered one morning to have breakfast.

Having bought himself some tea and toast and looking for a place to sit, Cem saw Emre sitting alone in a corner and went to meet him.

"Hey Emre, what's up, are you okay," he said and sitting next to him. Emre looked listless and angry. Staring at Cem's face, he said,

"You be happy, that would be enough for all of us," and turned his head the other way. Cem said,

"What does that mean?", trying to make sense of his words.

"Both Pelin and Alya. One woman is not enough for our man."

"Do you hear what you are saying?" said Cem, annoyed.

"You're an asshole!" hissed Emre, jumping to his feet. Now as they were looking eye to eye by knitting their brows,

"Besides, you're not ashamed to handle both Pelin and Alya," cried Emre.

"Hey, look at me!" said Cem, grabbing Emre's collar. While Emre was trying to save his collar from Cem's hands, he kept yelling,

"Because you gave Alya hope, she never looked at me," and Cem said,

"Shut up your mouth! Stop yelling!" his hands still on his collar, trying to pull him outside. Then he took Emre outside by holding his arm. By taking him to a quiet corner of the cafeteria's garden, he said,

"Now tell me your problem, let's hear what it is," standing in front of him.

"Hasan told me that you are in love with Alya," Emre said.

Now, Cem understood. When he and Hasan went out one night, they drank alcohol and had a deep conversation, including their private lives. He had shared with Hasan how he had buried his love in his heart and that the one he loved had gone to someone else. He told him that he could not get over her and that was in a lot of pain. Thinking that he would keep it to himself, Cem had told Hasan about Alya, and how he had to bury his love for her in his heart.

"It's not what you think," said Cem, trying to keep his calm.

"Alya keeps me distant because she knows this," said Emre. Cem shook his head helplessly, thinking about what he should tell Emre.

"I should have known when I asked you for help and you said 'don't get me involved, handle it yourself'," Emre said. Just as Cem said,

"Emre, look!" and tried to explain, Emre said,

"You didn't want Alya to be with me, you wanted to bench her because you thought you could be with her if things didn't work out with Pelin..." so Cem couldn't stand it anymore and punched Emre in the jaw with all his might. Losing his balance, Emre fell to the ground on his back. People in the cafeteria started to watch them, there was panic among those who saw the incident, and some people ran to Emre's help to pick him up from the ground.

"God damn you, you idiot!" said Cem, walking out of the cafeteria and rubbing his hand.

Jealousy had blinded Emre, and he even risked destroying their friendship for many years for Alya. It meant that he saw Cem as the reason for Alya's refusal, and he blamed him for believing things he made up in his head.

The two never met later and changed their way when they saw each other, thus ending their friendship for many years.

BEING A BROTHER REQUIRES RESPONSIBILITY

27) CEM AND PELİN'S MARRIAGE… 1992

When Cem graduated from the faculty as a young, handsome doctor, he didn't see Alya for a long time. Cem did not dare to call her, he buried all his feelings in his heart and went to Çankırı for his compulsory service that was required by the state. He worked there for about a year, and Pelin was always there with him. The preparations for starting a family in Çankırı, the families' meeting each other, the engagement, and the wedding, all happened within a year.

Pelin had a sister, whom she said she did not like at every opportunity because she thought she was a quarrelsome person. For Pelin, who was always having arguments with her parents, marriage was actually salvation. Having to live in the same house with them for a while after graduation turned Pelin's life into a nightmare; she wanted to get married without waiting for Cem's compulsory service to end.

Cem completed his specialization in Adana a short time after getting married, returning to his homeland years after where he spent his childhood, where his parents lived, and started working as an assistant at the Orthopedics

Clinic of Çukurova University. His uncle and aunts welcomed Cem warmly. The person they were proud of had become a grown man, got married, and received his specialization education in the city where they lived.

It was the year Yiğit graduated from high school when they came to Adana, and they found themselves involved in Yiğit's problems. The fact that Yiğit could not stay out of trouble due to drug things forced Cem to give his brother financial and moral support in this regard. Cem was also the first person Füsun called when she needed help with Yiğit's problems.

Her husband's fondness for his family began to bother Pelin over time. Especially the thought that Yiğit could not take care of himself and Cem would have to deal with him for the rest of his life made her uneasy. She could not understand why they always called Cem for help when there were his uncle and aunts, and she did not hesitate to start a fight about this issue.

A TRAUMA CAN REVEAL AN EXISTING DISEASE

28) ZEYNEP IS DIAGNOSED WITH BIPOLAR DISORDER... 1992

Zeynep's symptoms started to insidiously appear in the middle of her second year at the Fine Arts Academy, which she attended with great enthusiasm. Her mental state was now slowly signaling the situation. Füsun felt that Zeynep's experiences were not normal when she was unable to think logically, when she was too lethargic to move even one arm, or when she had a sudden onset of insomnia. Zeynep sometimes walked like a sleepwalker, didn't talk much, and stared blankly like a drug user. As a physician, she was aware that Zeynep would be diagnosed with a serious illness, but as a mother, it was very difficult for Füsun to accept this fact.

As months passed by and these symptoms started to appear, her own psychiatrist, Dr. Serpil, would begin to have doubts and of course, share them with Füsun. With the long-term follow-up and the findings she obtained, the event that confirmed her strong suspicions about the diagnosis was that Zeynep found herself on the streets one night for no reason.

After a night of arguing with her mother, Zeynep left the

house early before her mother woke up. She hadn't slept all night. She hadn't been eating properly for a long time and had stopped taking her medications for a few weeks. Dr. Serpil had changed her medications, but she had refused to take them, telling her mother that they did not make her feel good.

This morning, she was feeling very restless and irritable; thoughts were crowding her mind without giving her a rest. She left home so early that the public transportation service had not even begun their daily rides.

It was a cold October morning in Adana. She had run out to the street without putting on something warm. She was walking with her arms folded across her chest and she was terribly cold. She wandered aimlessly in the streets for a long time until the class hour. She saw stray dogs trying to find something to eat in the empty streets, and maybe three or five people who had left their house to go to work, who all stared at Zeynep as if they had seen something weird. They probably couldn't understand why this shivering girl was out at this early hour. One of them harassed her by his looks so much that she had shouted angrily,

"What are you looking at? Is there something weird?". The man said, "God… Is she crazy…" as he went on his way.

At that time, Zeynep had no fear of anyone or anything; she was unhappy, hopeless, and angry. She had walked for such a long time in the streets of Adana that she realized she had already missed her class when she looked at her wristwatch. She wasn't in the mood to go to class anyway, nor to see anyone… As she walked aimlessly, she got a sudden flash of inspiration and decided to go to Mersin.

She slowly walked towards Adana Bus Station. Before buying a ticket for the bus to Mersin, she went to the kiosk and had a little shopping. Asking the seller for a plastic bag, she filled it with biscuits, bubble gum, fruit juice, wafers, a few magazines on subjects that did not interest her, chocolate, water, and similar other things. With the plastic bag in her hand, full of unnecessary things she would probably not even eat, she went to buy a ticket to Mersin. Since there was still time for the bus to leave, she sat on the bench there, opened one of the biscuit packages she had bought trying to eat it, and began to wait. She waited, not knowing why she was going there or to whom, when she would be back, and why she had bought those groceries and magazines. It was as if she lost touch with the concepts of place and time; she acted without thinking, did not feel the need to question things as if she was getting orders from an unknown person, and she just obeyed them.

She had only eaten two biscuits when she realized the bus was about to leave. After sitting in her seat on the bus, she slept for about two hours in total during the trip, until the bus attendant woke her up in Mersin. She got off the bus at Mersin Bus Station, where she opened his eyes and looked around. She idly stood there and looked around, not knowing what to do. Then she decided to walk and left the bus station with the big plastic bag in her hand.

Late in the evening, Füsun was not worried first, since Zeynep had a habit of coming home late in the evenings. As the hours passed by and she still didn't show up, she slowly started to worry. After waiting a while longer, trying to stay positive -she began to panic now- she couldn't stand it any longer and decided to call Sinan. When she heard the words,

"We haven't met today, Mrs. Füsun," and hearing the same thing from her close friend Aycan, she began to panic more. When Aycan said,

"She didn't even come to school today," Füsun suddenly felt helpless. She sat in the chair with the pain in her heart and started praying, wishing that nothing bad would happen to her.

It was already past midnight, Füsun had called all the hospitals in Adana with Yiğit, but found nothing. They also informed the police station, they said that they would inform them when they have information, and added they had to come to the police station the next day to file the report. They also said that the person had to be unreachable for a certain period to file a missing person application.

Füsun suddenly realized that she had to call Emin as well. Maybe he could do something; he still had a social circle there, after all. Risking everything, she dialed Emin's house in Urla; Gül answered the phone. The fact that she had to talk to Gül poured fuel on the fire. Gül was added to her past experience with Zeynep flashing before her eyes, and she felt pain in her heart. Füsun was crying silently, not knowing what to say, standing there with the receiver in her hand and unable to stop tears from rolling down her cheeks. She didn't know if she was crying for Zeynep or what she had been through in the past, they were all mixed up. She was under a torrent of emotions.

Her children had talked about Gül after coming back from Izmir each year. Füsun thought about Gül and her daughters for a moment. She had seen a lot of photos of them together taken during the summer. She had heard a lot of stories about her, but she had not heard her voice for years. At those times when she looked at those photos, she realized with pain that witnessing the happiness of Gül, Emin, and the children was underlining her own unhappiness.

She couldn't pull herself together for a while even after she hung up, but she couldn't think about that right now. Her daughter was missing and she was worried. She talked to Sinan a few more times at night, who started to wait anxiously as well. He also looked at the places where Zeynep was likely to go, but could not find her. Füsun did not sleep until the morning, smoked a lot of cigarettes, and drank a lot of coffee. At sunrise, as she was snoozing on the sofa with her head on the side, she woke up with her son's voice,

"Mom, come on, get up and go to bed." Seeing that it was nine o'clock, she asked, "No news from Zeynep?" trying to collect herself. "No, mom," said Yiğit.

She got up from her seat and headed to the bathroom, saying, "God, give me strength." Füsun started to listen with great attention when she heard the phone ringing while she was in the bathroom.

Realizing that the person Yiğit was talking to was his father, she continued to wash her face slowly.

"My father was also trying to reach my sister through his acquaintances at the police station," Yiğit said after hanging up the phone. After Füsun got out of the bathroom, she said,

"I hope they find her," and headed to the kitchen to make some tea. She kept thinking about what else she could do as she poured water into the teapot.

Hoping that she might find something, Füsun called a few more friends of Zeynep, who came to her mind late at night but could not call at that late hour. They had not heard from her either. The situation had already been reported to the police. She didn't want to spend another day waiting around smoking and drinking tea all day.

Füsun, who couldn't sleep properly all night, was snoozing on the sofa and she jumped at the sound of the phone ring. When she excitedly picked up the phone, she heard Sinan's cheerful voice saying,

"Hello, Mrs. Füsun, I found out where Zeynep is," a smile, something she had forgotten for a long time, settled on her face.

"Thank God, thank God," she said, her words following one after the other. Then she asked, "Where is she? Is she okay?".

"Yeah, she's fine. She went to Mersin to a friend of ours. My friend realized that she wasn't well and called me saying 'you should come and pick her up, she isn't well enough to go back herself.' Now I'm going to Mersin to pick her up. I thought I'd let you know so you don't have to worry anymore."

"Thank you very much, my child, you are very thoughtful. You want me to come?" asked Füsun.

"It's not necessary. I'll pick her up and bring her home. Don't worry. I'll talk to her a little on the way too. Let's see what her reason was for not letting us know," said Sinan as if he was going to call Zeynep to account for.

"Thank you very much, my child. We're troubling you too," said Füsun again.

"Please, it's no trouble at all," said Sinan in a respectful voice.

"Okay, thank you, again," said Füsun, and hung up. She didn't know whether to laugh or cry, but she definitely felt relieved. Füsun was sure that this thing Zeynep had done, who had previously attempted suicide and was diagnosed with 'childhood depression' at the time due to the traumas she had to go through, had nothing to do with depression anymore.

"God bless us," she said, sitting on the sofa. She called Yiğit and asked him to inform his father that Zeynep was found.

Neither Füsun nor Yiğit and Sinan could ask her anything, as Zeynep gave a definite ultimatum that she was not to be asked anything after her return. But it was clear that Zeynep was not well at all. She looked very tired, she was looking at their faces in a meaningless way without reacting to the questions they asked and the words they spoke. Zeynep did not get out of bed for a long time after she returned from that journey, the reason of which no one could understand. She wanted to sleep all the time and refused to eat. Her self-care had diminished, and she had difficulty communicating with the person in front of her.

She could not resist Sinan's insistence and words of love any longer and finally agreed to go to her psychiatrist. Dr. Serpil, who closely followed the strict anamnesis, the findings, and Zeynep's feelings and experiences, diagnosed Zeynep's illness as 'bipolar disorder,' which is characterized by periods of exuberance and periods of inactivity.

She added, "We call periods of exuberance manic periods, and periods of inactivity depression periods."

"Events such as a death in the family, losing a job, giving birth, divorce or moving can trigger an already existing disease," she continued her speech.

Zeynep did not want to accept her diagnosis at first, and she tried to show what was going on around her as the reason that she was in this state, behaving in this way. Her symptoms improved shortly after she began using the medication Dr. Serpil prescribed.

But now she was diagnosed with a disease that would be with her for the rest of her life. It was such a disease that if she embraced it and accepted to live with it, life would be relatively easier, but if she denied it and refused to fulfill her part, her life would be unbearable. She had to take her medication regularly and stay away from events that would create tension. While periods of exuberance and depression were rare at the beginning of the disease, the frequency of these periods would, unfortunately, increase as the years passed. The doctor emphasized that support from the family and those around her was very important in the beginning and continuing the treatment of this disease, so Füsun and Sinan would have a huge role in this as well.

During manic periods, Zeynep was very enthusiastic and energetic, talked a lot, and spent a lot of money. In this period when she hit the peak of entertainment with her crazy plans, parties, and trips, she would always be surrounded by friends. Zeynep would become very popular during those time since she would entertain people and spare no expense. At those times, there would be a decrease in her need for sleep and an increase in her alcohol use.

During the depressive period, on the other hand, she would become withdrawn, and she felt guilt and regret. In the past, her activities would not give her pleasure, she would have pain in her body without a reason, and she would constantly whine and complain.

At the slightest thing told against her and the positive or negative emotion she felt, she would start to cry, could not eat, and could not sleep properly. At such times, her pessimistic look at life would prevent her from getting pleasure from anything.

Zeynep used her medication regularly at university and the extreme symptoms between the two periods were not very apparent, but as years would pass by, some parameters of this disease would affect her a lot.

EMOTIONAL NEEDS OF A CHILD MUST BE MET

29) YİĞİT MEETS ECSTASY... 1993

Yiğit found out that the math teacher was not in the study center, so he was sitting in the cafeteria watching the rain while waiting for the next class. The rain was pouring outside. He was lost in thought about the big argument he had with Zeynep last night.

He had argued with his sister as long as he could remember. He never stopped supporting Zeynep when she needed help, but he was always met with rudeness and insults in return. For some reason, anything he did or said was enough to bother Zeynep.

"Hey man, are you okay?" Mustafa said, throwing himself into the chair next to him.

Yiğit replied, "The teacher did not come, I am waiting for the next class."

"You look upset," said Mustafa, smiling.

Yiğit sighed, saying, "I don't want to go to class at all." Mustafa stared at him for a long time, and then put a yellow pill with a picture of a bird next to his hand on the table. When he saw Yiğit looking at him with questioning eyes, he quietly said,

"Trust me, there's nothing to worry about," putting his

hand on Yiğit's hand. At that time, someone called for Mustafa. Mustafa got up, shouting at the person calling him,

"Okay, okay, I'm coming!". Leaning towards Yiğit, he said, "I have to go, brother, see you later" and left.

Yiğit was left along with the pill in front of him. He more or less understood what had happened, he had heard it before from his teachers and his mother. But they usually talked about it with a warning attitude. "Be careful", "It's dangerous! Stay away!", "Don't do it!" and the sort.

He thought for a long time, looking at the pill in front of him, wondering how it would affect him. He eventually took the pill with the excitement of taking a risk, popped it in his mouth, and swallowed it with the water on the table. Half an hour after entering the class, Yiğit began to feel so good. His tiredness, distress, and pessimism had vanished. He felt intense happiness and a strong desire to see his mother. All he wanted to do at the moment was to see his mother and hug her. The strange thing was that his interest in his class increased as well, and he attentively listened to and understood what the teacher was telling. As soon as the class was over, he took the minibus and went home. When he got home, he was about to insert the key in the lock when he heard voices from the inside and paused. Zeynep and his mother were both shouting:

"You are irresponsible!" Füsun was saying or rather yelling.

"And you? Are you the picture of responsibility, do you fulfill all your responsibilities towards your children!" replied Zeynep.

"You have to plan your future and take responsibility for it," Füsun was saying.

"And you just want your children to get off your back. 'Oh, they should take responsibility, leave me alone.' You think being a mother only means giving money to your children,"

Zeynep was saying.

"I have never seen anyone as selfish and quarrelsome as you in my life," Füsun said.

"Is it because you are not quarrelsome at all that my father left us all; you couldn't even stop him from running away"

Zeynep always reminded her mother that if she had been a proper wife and stayed with her father, none of this would have happened. Her mother was entirely responsible for their situation, she said. If Füsun had not gotten a divorce from Emin, she would have been a role model to Zeynep. She had caused her father to go away with someone else, and therefore no one had the right to blame Zeynep.

Yiğit did not enter, he collapsed on the stairs in front of the door and sat there for a while.

The voices coming from inside did not seem to stop. Zeynep started to cry again. She was crying loudly and shouting at the same time. This was what she did when she got angry, her best card. He hated her sister. He didn't know how long he had sat there. Then he slowly got up and quickly descended the stairs, exited the apartment, and started briskly walking in the streets with his hands in his pockets.

He walked and thought for hours on the streets all around Adana. Dam Road, Sular, Station Square, Ziya Paşa Boulevard, Abidinpaşa, Atatürk Street... His mind was so clear, his despair was so much that he couldn't control the thoughts in his head, he couldn't put them in order.

He was grown up now and he had to be able to take care of himself. He would be strong and would not let any disaster affect him. He made a lot of decisions during his walk. But 'How strong could he be?', 'How would he be able to take care of himself?', 'How would he be able to fend himself in face of disasters?'. He wasn't able to answer those questions, and he never would be. Nor would he have the power to implement the decisions he took. He was thinking as he walked, taking decisions, never feeling tired...

In the meantime, Mustafa and -his so-called brother- Yiğit began to meet more often. He was appearing in front of Yiğit when he least expected it, he was speaking out of both sides of his mouth; he was also bringing him pills known as ecstasy from time to time. These were colorful pills with pictures of butterflies, birds, stars, hearts, and smiling faces on them. These pills made Yiğit feel so good; his self-confidence skyrocketed. Listening to lectures and concentrating became easier. Although he slept less, he felt fit and did not feel tired at all.

Yiğit realized over time that he felt much better with those pills, so he began to find them when he wanted some, or at least learn how to find them. At first, Mustafa brought him some whenever he wanted. When Mustafa was not around – sometimes Mustafa disappeared for days – he sent a message to him through his friends, stating that he wanted 'colored candy'. Mustafa used to bring it himself, but when he wasn't there, he began to send them via other kids.

Thanks to Emin, who tried to make up for his absence by sending a lot of money, and Füsun, who did not want his son to suffer financially, Yiğit had no financial problems and he was able to get any amount of stimulant drugs he wanted.

Having continued the same study center for two years, Yiğit's circle of friends grew bigger towards the end of high school, and he got to know a lot of people thanks to Mustafa, but his social relations were very problematic. He continued to go to the Study Center after school, but he was not attending the classes regularly anymore. He was mostly on the streets now. He had made friends outside of school and study center too, and most of them were kids who had nothing to do with classes or school. Children of that age also began smoking cigarettes, which they believed was proof that they had grown up.

After Yiğit got used to taking ecstasy, he started to feel irritated if he didn't take more after a few days. He began to flare up with anger suddenly due to ordinary events, he would involve in fights for nothing, and he began to feel tense due to trivial issues.

At such moments, all he wanted was to find and take those pills again. When he couldn't find some, he couldn't wake up in the morning and was reluctant to go to school. This situation infuriated Füsun, who found it unacceptable that Yiğit didn't go to school because he didn't want to, making her angry in such mornings. Even if he went to school, his mind was all over the place and he could not focus on any subject.

As he developed tolerance over time, the duration of the effect of ecstasy began to get shorter. He needed stimulant drugs that would make him feel better and last longer. His friends had given him marijuana, saying that it was not addictive, and he believed them. Yiğit contented himself for a long time with marijuana until the types and amounts of the substances he would use in the future increased.

Deprived of his father's love and his mother's attention, Yiğit grew up thinking that no matter how hard he tried, he could not do anything right, that something was always missing in his life. He constantly felt his father's absence, and when he felt insignificant and worthless, he clung to drugs. But these drugs did not meet his emotional needs, on the contrary, they were raising these feelings of emptiness every day.

Yiğit, who hit the streets, made friends with vagrants, and did not care about his classes anymore, could not pass the university exam the year he graduated from high school. Füsun made a mistake about Yiğit as well, and could not prevent his life from slipping away before her eyes. She had dealt with Yiğit until that disastrous day arrived and knocked on the door, and she had to sacrifice a lot of herself and her life.

EVERY PERSON'S LIFE IS THE RESULT OF THEIR CHOICES

30) DILA STARTS TO WEAR HIJAB... 1993

Dila started to wear a hijab during the summer holiday in the third year of high school. Of course, she did not make this decision overnight; she had been thinking about it for a year or two, but she couldn't dare to do it earlier. She would later tell his mother what made it easier for her to take this decision; it was a dream she had one night in which she was 'waiting in line in front of hell'. After this dream, she bought herself a hijab with pastel colors such as peachy and light blue. She would keep this hijab for the rest of her life as a memory of the time she started wearing the hijab.

Dila had already learned how to perform the ritual prayers of Islam from Sevinç. Every day after school, she had been praying at appropriate times, but she did not dare to start wearing hijab until then. Prayer had a great influence on her decision to start wearing the hijab. She believed she was complete with the hijab, and felt that the more she came into contact with God, the closer she got to him. Dila had asked her mother and Alya for their opinions in many decisions she took, but she made this decision by herself. It was as if this decision was a rebellion against her family, her mother, and the world and a way of proving herself...

Dila was very happy following the rules of God, felt

completely peaceful perhaps for the first time in her life, with the peace of mind of someone who fulfills the duties given by God, and the reward of going to heaven in return.

When Alper, who called Gül to give the news of the death of a mutual friend in Adana, said that Dila started wearing hijab, Gül was very surprised and could not believe her ears. After hanging up the phone, she remained silent for a while with the receiver in hand, trying to comprehend what Alper had just said, and the past flashing before her eyes like a film strip.

Dila was Gül's self-confident, good-hearted, quiet daughter. A timid, stubborn child who always approached life sensitively and sought approval from others.

In fact, at the beginning of high school, when she came to Izmir for summer vacation, Gül had realized that her choices of conversation topics were different than usual. She remembered that Dila talked a lot about such spiritual matters and warned her several times that she was sinning. At that moment, she thought that she was influenced by her grandmother and that this might be reflected in her speech; so, she wasn't wrong then. She also knew that Alper's second wife, Sevinç, also had a conservative background; she was probably influenced by her as well. On the same day, Gül spoke to Alper for the second time:

"Was she influenced by your wife or her grandmother in this decision?" she asked.

"She made this decision herself," replied Alper.

When Gül said, "For God's sake! What free will are you talking about! Dila is only seventeen..." raising her voice, Alper replied,

"Exactly, no one can influence her, she is a big girl," ironically. Gül, with the shock of the event, shouted,

"But that is not possible," and Alper calmly replied,

"Dila can do whatever she wants, no one can interfere."

Gül overreacted at first, yelling and shouting in the room by herself after hanging up the phone.

Her first thought was 'I shouldn't have let her go to Adana'. Of course, she knew how important the attitude of the parents was in the decisions of children. Growing up as a child with a weak spirit and body, Dila also had a greater potential to be affected by her environment compared to Alya.

She also thought about whether she had a share in Dila's decision, 'Where did I go wrong?' she asked herself for a long time. After blaming Alper's new wife and her ex-mother-in-law, who never loved her and who she thought were influencing Dila, Gül slowly began to accept the truth.

However, the question of whether things could have been different if she could wind back the clock would still haunt her from time to time.

After wandering around like this for a few days, angry and confused, she finally decided to talk to Dila. She waited for a few days after hearing it from Alper, fearing she might say things she doesn't mean with the shock of the incident, and she decided to call after calming down. She first called Alya and asked,

"Did you know about this?" directly.

"She called me, yes, but she said 'I began to wear hijab,' she didn't say 'I'm going to wear hijab'," Alya replied. This made Gül even more upset:

"Then I was the only one who didn't know," she said.

"When I found out, she had already begun wearing hijab long ago and I thought you should hear it from her, not me."

"You are her elder sister, you should have tried to persuade her otherwise, or you should have called me"

"Mom, believe me, you wouldn't be able to do anything. She had already made her decision," said Alya.

"Of course, she didn't dare to tell me. Because she knew I was going to pester her."

"Probably mom," Alya laughed sarcastically on the other end of the phone.

When Gül, who later called Dila, asked:

"Why did you do such a thing, darling?" Dila responded,

"This is not something to talk about on the phone; we should talk face to face. Believe me, my reasons will put you at ease too," preventing Gül from speaking further and asking questions.

Gül realized how determined Dila was; she realized that whatever she would say would be meaningless and she did not bring up this subject again. Dila was determined, and Gül knew her daughter enough to know that once she decided on something, it was impossible to convince her otherwise.

In time, Gül accepted the situation as well; there was nothing she could do. Her daughter had made her decision through her own free will and wanted to live like this. She never attempted to call Dila, talk to her, and persuade her. When they got together much later, she witnessed how much she had matured, saying good and hopeful things about the future. As a mother, her duty was to pray 'I hope she will be happy for life' and send a positive message to the universe. When they got together, what Dila told her, "I respect people's lives and decisions, and I expect people to respect my life and my decisions," would always be in the back of her mind. After all, everyone lived the life they chose…

After graduating from high school, Dila got into Çukurova University Faculty of Theology, which she wanted to study the most. After she graduated, she married a pious, wealthy man from the family circle of her stepmother Sevinç, who introduced her to him. Her husband, who engaged in trade, treated Dila well and provided the necessary money for his family. Dila did not work after getting married and preferred to raise her children herself. But at the time, of course, they did not know what the time would bring, how a person's destiny might change in the matter of a moment...

LIFE MAY CHANGE WITHIN A MOMENT IN A WAY YOU NEVER EXPECTED

31) YİĞİT GOES TO JAIL... 1993

As Yiğit's drug problem got worse, he began to less frequently go home. He was mostly on the streets now, waking up in different places, not remembering how he got there or how he went to sleep. Dila, who went to the same school, saw Yiğit's doom but it was not just her witnessing it. His mother didn't like his vagrant and wayward behavior either. His grades were getting worse and worse, and his teachers were asking, 'What happened to Yiğit?'.

Füsun had never even thought that her son might be involved with drugs, so she did not even suspect it because it never occurred to her. But that night when she had to get out of bed in the dead of night to go to the police station, she finally learned the terrible truth she had a hard time accepting, and she didn't even suspect, because she didn't think her son would ever do it. It was one of the nights Yiğit said,

"I'll stay at my friend's tonight," and didn't come home. Zeynep was having trouble sleeping and she had just fallen asleep when Füsun shook her violently to wake her up. She saw her mother in front of her with tears in her eyes and jumped out of bed in fear.

"What happened?" she asked her mother. Füsun couldn't speak, she was just crying. As Zeynep kept yelling,

"Mom, what happened? Speak to me, for God's sake!" She swallowed and said,

"They called from the police station."

"And?" said Zeynep, looking at her mother with sleepy eyes.

"They took Yiğit into custody," said Füsun. Zeynep hastily got out of the bed. She fearfully asked,

"What did he do to be taken into custody?". Her mother said,

"I don't know, they just told me to come," answering Zeynep's question.

It was December in Adana with a penetrating cold. Füsun and Zeynep went to the police station in the middle of the night, wrapped in their coats and scarves, not knowing what to expect. When they entered the police station, they felt warmth on their faces, and they directly headed to the officer on duty to introduce themselves. The officer told them to wait and disappeared into his chief's office. Another police officer showed them seats and offered them tea. They were halfway through their tea when the first police officer came back and said that his chief was waiting for them. They walked in with worry and fear clearly visible in their eyes. The station chief, who learned that Füsun was a doctor, said,

"Welcome, Mrs. Doctor," welcoming them to his office and showing them the chairs. After the brief small talk, the chief informed them that Yiğit was unfortunately involved in a fight and his nose might be broken.

"We will make a decision based on the assault report from the hospital," he said.

They waited anxiously in the pale, whitewashed police

station, with a loose light bulb hanging from the ceiling. During that long, nervous, and sleepy wait, the police officer said,

"We suspected that your son might be using stimulant drugs, and we sent a urine sample to the forensics for investigation, the results will be out in a few days."

Fortunately, they learned that the battered person did not file a complaint when the assault report arrived. In his first incident, Yiğit had gotten away with a few days of jail time. That's when Füsun found out that Yiğit was using those drugs. They were unaware of this until that night, but over time, they would be accustomed to Yiğit's getting involved with violent incidents and being taken into custody, arriving home with his face battered, not coming home for days without letting them know, and such incidents.

RIGHT COMMUNICATION OPENS EVERY DOOR

32) ZEYNEP INVITES SİNAN TO DINNER WITH HER FATHER… 1993

Zeynep's relationship with Sinan started at university and continued for a long time with its ups and downs after they graduated. Sinan was always there for Zeynep during and after she opened her painting studio. He always handled all the bureaucratic and technical things and errands that needed to be done by his practicality. Sinan was already a cheerful and lively person, and he would surrender himself to Zeynep during her manic periods. During those periods, they would have the time of their lives, never standing still, going everywhere in Adana. During Zeynep's depressive and unhappy periods, on the other hand, he would do his best to support her.

Sinan also tried to establish good relations with Zeynep's family, and he insisted to meet her mother at the beginning of their relationship; he used every opportunity to that end. One day, while they were at a friend's house, Füsun, who knew that Zeynep was there, called her friend's house and found her there. When Sinan hear Zeynep's voice saying,

"Ugh mom! You always do the same thing?",

"Just think about where you've been,"

"It's your irresponsibility, there is nothing I can do, sorry!" he understood that Mrs. Füsun lost her key and was locked out of the house. He remembered that Zeynep talked about something like this before. As Zeynep was about to hang up the phone after grumbling a bit more, Sinan jumped up to his feet and left, saying,

"I'll bring the locksmith to your mother," walking out the door. Zeynep was stunned with the receiver in her hand, and said, "Mom, wait there, Sinan is coming with the locksmith" with a surprised voice.

Yet another day, when a water pipe burst and flooded Füsun's house, he went over with a few people, sent the carpets floating in the water to be washed, had the whole house cleaned, and took care of everything by the evening. She believed that Sinan valued her daughter and did his best for her happiness; there was no reason for Füsun not to love Sinan.

When Emin came to Adana from time to time, he would call Zeynep, and the father and daughter would go out to dinner, happy to see each other.

In fact, both of them wondered how the other one was doing, and they would secretly watch each other while chatting throughout dinner.

During a week when Emin came to Adana due to his illness, Zeynep invited Sinan to their dinner after asking her father's permission. It was his right to know who her daughter was with. Emin wanted to get to know Sinan better and learn about his thoughts and perspective on life, so he started conversations on various topics during the dinner and examined his reactions. Sinan had something to say about everything and he loved to talk, so he did his best to impress Emin.

Emin's old friend Taner was a senior manager at the newspaper 'Yeni Adana', where Sinan was working. The next day, Taner was delighted to see his old friend Emin, whom he had not seen for a long time, at the door of his office.

He got up from his seat to hug his old friend and asked, "What brought you here?" The two friends who had seen each other all the time when Emin used to live in Adana had missed each other a lot and they lost track of time while talking. They had agreed to meet in the evening to continue their conversation, which was left unfinished due to colleagues entering Taner's room. During these conversations, Emin asked him what he thought about Sinan. Taner said that he was very good at his job, and his writing was very powerful and effective. He said, "If you're asking me as a journalist, I can say that he is an excellent journalist with a good background."

"But unfortunately, I can't say the same things for his personality," he added.

At that time, Zeynep was happy to see that her father was trying to get to know Sinan and they got along, and she didn't yet know that not only her father but everyone in her life would get to know Sinan in the future and they would not be happy about it...

FRIENDS ARE ESSENTIAL FOR HAPPINESS

33) GÜL'S MEDITATION GROUP... 1987-2001

No one was better than Gül at attracting attention in any room she entered. Calmly speaking and attentively listening to anyone who had something to say without discriminating young or old, rich or poor, and showing that she valued them were the main factors that made her so lovable. Shortly after moving to Urla, Gül, who believed that one's life should not only be about home, children, and spouse and that pursuing happiness is important, had built herself a social circle in which she could blow off steam.

According to her, she had to ensure her own happiness first to be able to make her family happy. At first, she started to meet a doctor friend from her workplace with whom she got closer over time. After meeting this friend for a long time, she invited Derya to one of those meetings, who was a high school friend she saw in Urla by chance. The last addition to this group of friends was the person her high school friend introduced to them. Forming a group of friends when they could instantly agree to meet whenever one of them asked, eating together, and having long conversations, did not happen at once, it took time.

The group consisted of a housewife, a manager, and two doctors, and some of them were interested in yoga, some in traveling; some talked as if they had found the meaning of life, and some were becoming more mature by learning from their experiences from their lovers which they changed a lot... Some were making light of life in order to be happy, some assumed a humble attitude when there was an incident, and some fought to the last drop of their blood. Each had something to learn from the other; there was always something to think about, something to be sad about, something to be happy about, and something to be angry about. There was even a person who tried to join the group but was not successful. They believed this person was not honest and they ruled her out.

There are moments when a person is confused, does not know what to do, and really needs help from someone. At such moments, the 'Come on Group' would come to the rescue. This group was formed with effort after Gül came to Urla, but it would continue for about fifteen years with meetings with short or long breaks, with all members or with some missing.

One summer day, when all the children were in Urla, Zeynep did not come to dinner in the evening, and she came home very late. It was the summer when Zeynep was sixteen years old, and cell phones, which would assume an important place in people's lives in the future, were not yet invented in those years. Gül did not want to worry Emin, who was working a shift. She got into her car and started looking for Zeynep, trying to guess where young people might go. She saw Zeynep from afar in one of those fast food places, which were a few then, with a spacious environment and music that young people enjoyed. There were two other girls with her and they were eating food. She waited outside for a while, then asked a waiter to call Zeynep outside. Surprised to see her, Zeynep asked,

"What are you doing here?" rolling her eyes. Gül said,

"We were worried about you."

"I found my school friend Ece from Adana and I'm going to have dinner with her," said Zeynep.

"We wouldn't be worried if you'd let us know."

"Are you really worried about me, or are you questioning me now because you don't know what to tell my father if something happens to me?" she said, making Gül angry.

"Do you hear what you're saying?" she said, trying to stay calm. Zeynep must have realized that she had gone too far, so she said,

"Okay, I'll be home in an hour," and walked away. Gül got extremely angry and felt helpless about what to do; she could only think 'How rebellious'.

After returning home, she sat in the living room and patiently waited for her to come home so she could talk to her; she tried to talk to her but she was unsuccessful when she came back home three hours later. Zeynep went to her room, saying she was tired, without even going into the living room.

When Gül told about this to the 'Come on Group', the group members and they talked about it from different perspectives, they concluded that Gül needed to empathize with her, and it was decided that tolerance would be the best approach for Gül in this case. Anything else would only harm her…

Gül also shared with the group many of her problems with Emin and asked for her friends' opinions. She had cried at the 'Come on' table, about Emin accusing Gül because of her friend Erhan. Of course, she couldn't accept such an accusation, but a few words from her friends and their jokes made it a little more tolerable and relieved Gül, even though it was difficult for her.

Again, at that table, Emin's tendency to blame other people because of things that happened as a result of his actions was discussed, and they had concluded that it was because of things like 'general male character', 'men who do not grow up', and 'men who need to appear strong in society'. It was also this group that convinced Gül to be temperate and sensitive towards her daughter when Dila started to wear hijab. The unfortunate events of her childhood friend Derya, Yiğit's unsalvageable future, Alya's hopeless love, the phone call from Emin's ex-wife Füsun in the middle of the night were all discussed in this group. Gül's 'Come on Group' was a bit of escape, a little break from all the children in those hot, suffocating summer days. The subject the women in the group couldn't close would be opened with the breeze coming from the windows in their hearts, discussed at this table; they would be talked over sometimes with longing, sometimes with anger, and sometimes with sadness.

'Come on Group' met for years, never stopped getting together, despite the terrible event that deeply affected all of them, until the second person had to leave Urla... They lost one of their dearest friends to colon cancer. Even though there was always sadness - in every meeting, there was always a drink in honor of that person - they continued to meet. They had never left their dear friend alone during her illness. They did their best to make her life easier and gave moral support to her family.

After that loss, which was very sad and affected all of them deeply, their meetings gradually became infrequent after another friend's son got into university in Istanbul and she left with him. But one needed supportive friends to blow off steam with, to spend a good time together, and to see different perspectives to know oneself better. The person who had these things is able to have a positive outlook on life; just like Gül...

SOMETIMES IT HURTS TO REMEMBER THE PAST

34) FÜSUN TALKS TO GÜL ON THE PHONE... 1992

At two o'clock in the night, when everyone was asleep, Gül woke up to the sound of the phone ringing. She quickly picked up the receiver to stop the sound from waking up the children. Her heart started beating very fast for the fear of hearing bad news. After a deep breath, in a barely audible voice, she said,

"Yes?". Gül's fear intensified when the person on the other end of the phone was silent. She decided that the person could not speak because they didn't dare to give the bad news, so she raised her voice a little and asked,

"Hello, who are you?" again. She was sure that she was going to hear something bad, and a lot of thoughts went through her mind in a matter of seconds.

It was Füsun on the other end of the phone who panicked when she heard Gül's voice and waited silently, not knowing what to say. In a weak voice that was hard to hear, she was only able to say,

"Hello!". She made the phone call despite knowing that Gül might pick up, but she still couldn't speak for a while because she was surprised and didn't know what to say.

The two friends had not heard each other's voices for a long time. Füsun had never wanted to see Gül; she was as angry with her as she was with Emin.

It was Gül's turn to be silent now, and she didn't know what to say, she couldn't speak. After getting over her fear and initial surprise, she said, "Hi! How are you?". Füsun ignored this and said,

"I need to talk to Emin, it's urgent, that's why I called at this hour. I need to talk to him right away, can you give him the phone?".

"Emin is not at home, he has a shift tonight," said Gül. Once again, there was silence. Since Füsun's voice sounded so bad on the phone, Gül understood that something was wrong. She thought that she needed to help her old friend, so she quickly said,

"I'll try to reach him somehow and have him call you." She felt that Füsun was crying. She couldn't stop her tears either as they started flowing down her cheeks. Deep down, she felt a pang in her heart; the pang of the good days they had in the past. Two women on two ends of the phone, two old friends, both crying now…

Gül reached Emin, explained the situation to him, and she told him to call Füsun. Calling Füsun without delay, Emin learned that Zeynep had not been seen for a whole day, they had not heard from her for a long time, they were very worried, and her friends did not know anything.

As Füsun, who had been weepy lately, told him the situation while crying with panic, there were moments when she couldn't speak and only her sobs could be heard on the phone. Füsun was a nervous wreck, she was feeling very helpless, and she could not control her tears. Emin told her that she should remain calm and tried to comfort her by saying:

"I'm sure she'll come home eventually, she's a strong girl, don't worry." He said that but he was worried as well.

After he hung up the phone, Emin felt sad while hearing Füsun's voice in that mood under those conditions. He sat in silence for a while, thinking about what to do. When he was able to collect his thoughts, he called some people he knew in Adana who could help, and he mobilized everyone he could. Then, he called Füsun almost every hour and kept asking if there were any news.

SOMETIMES IT MAY BE TOO LATE TO REPAIR THINGS

35) EMİN GOES TO ADANA FOR HIS SON... 1994

While they were going to the same high school, Dila was heartbroken whenever she saw Yiğit during breaktimes or after school because he looked so bad now. Whenever she asked him to share his problems with her, he said,

"It's nothing, I'm fine." Realizing that she could not help Yiğit in any way, Dila thought for a long time about what she could do, and in the end, she decided to call her mother to talk to Uncle Emin.

When Füsun found out that Yiğit had been taking stimulant drugs the day he was taken into custody, she called Emin the next day. When Emin found out what had happened, he had a very bad day, wandering around like a ghost all day long. On top of that, when Gül came home in the evening and told him what Dila had told her about Yiğit, Emin was shocked.

Not knowing what to do, Emin first thought about calling his brother who lived in Adana. He told him about the case and requested him to ask around about Yiğit.

"I will do what is required, trust me," said his brother Mustafa. Mustafa had strong connections, and after asking around, he said,

"Unfortunately, Yiğit is most likely taking drugs," and he was very surprised at what he found out as well. Moreover, Yiğit was not only using ecstasy, but also marijuana, as his mother guessed. Realizing with sadness that he had neglected his nephew and did not realize what was happening even though he was living so close to him, Mustafa would feel the sting of conscience for a long time.

After what he had heard, Emin's world came crushing down around him; and as a doctor, he painfully realized that it was unfortunately too late for those things that should have been done. He would always feel the pain in his heart because he wasn't there for Yiğit in his difficult times and didn't take care of him, and he would never be able to silence the voice of his conscience for the rest of his life.

After Yiğit graduated from high school, Emin took a long-term leave from work to be with his son and see if there was anything he could do and went to Adana, staying at the farmhouse that his brother managed.

He realized that his mother and siblings, whom he had last seen at the funeral when he lost his father two years ago, missed him very much. He too missed both his family and Adana very much. For the first time since marrying Gül, he questioned himself, "What am I doing in Izmir?" and painfully thought, "My land, my family are here, and where am I?" Emin was making plans to return to his hometown for good after many years, but at that moment he had no idea how and in what way he could do that. Moreover, his eldest son, Cem, would return to the city long before him, the city he had left years ago to receive his specialization.

While Emin was in Adana, he asked around about Yiğit's health, social circle, and friends, and tried to find out more about his social situation. He was already beginning to feel the pain of what was to come. Knowing that the sooner the treatment is started, the better the outcome will be, Emin talked to Füsun several times and asked her to help him. Füsun was aware of the ups and downs in Yiğit's life, and she said,

"I would do anything for him to get him back to his previous self," she said hopefully. She had made an appointment with the psychiatrist, hoping to give him some mental relief.

Emin brought Yiğit, who did not want to meet with his uncle and aunts even though they were in the same city, to the farmhouse, though by a little force, and hoped that a change of environment would be good for him. Unfortunately, the bond between Cem and his father's family did not happen with Yiğit. Unlike Cem, who preferred to spend most of his days with them when he came to Adana, he did not like the farm and his father's side of the family as much as Cem did. During his stay in Adana, Emin had put excessive pressure on Yiğit to receive treatment, especially for inpatient treatment. He was calling him frequently, asking to meet outside, but he had to exert a lot of effort to spend even one hour with him. Yiğit, on the other hand, hated that his father was trying to create opportunities to spend time with him, that he had to answer his questions all the time, and that he tried to paint the picture of a caring father.

Unable to convince Yiğit about the treatment, Emin had to return to İzmir after staying there for a long time.

YOUR CHILD IS THE ONLY PERSON WHOSE PAIN YOU WANT TO TAKE ON YOURSELF

36) YİĞİT GOES TO ANOTHER CITY FOR TREATMENT... 1994

It was a Sunday when Zeynep and Yiğit had a big argument again, when Zeynep said,

"I'm going to my friend," by crying, before she slammed the door and left. Yiğit was walking around in the house, swearing, throwing a glass to the door Zeynep slammed, the glass smashed to smithereens. Füsun had her hands on her mouth with panic, watching the scene with widened eyes. Such incidents became constant when the children were together. Both were temperamental; Füsun was afraid they might hurt each other. In those moments, she would be torn between them, feeling helpless.

When Zeynep left, Füsun took a deep breath and calmed down; then, she went to the other room to get the vacuum cleaner.

"You have an insufferable, psychopathic daughter," Yiğit said, raising his voice. Füsun nodded silently, busy picking up shards of glass from the ground. When Füsun was finished and went to Yiğit's room, she found him lying on the bed listening to music. Silently sitting on the sofa next to the bed and examining Yiğit's face, she said,

"You were such a sensitive kid when you were little, I tried so hard to keep you out of family turmoil." Yiğit silently looked into his mother's eyes, full of tears ready to flow, without saying anything.

"You were my youngest, but I used to benefit from your ideas the most, you know?" she said. She was trying to smile while wiping the tears that wet her cheek.

"You would try to support me with your little heart when I was sad, you would hug me, put your face on my neck and breathe in my scent."

"Yeah I remember. I used to think that there is no better smell in the world than the smell of my mother," said Yiğit without taking his eyes off his mother. Füsun, smiling with pain, said,

"I never knew you thought that way."

"I was very afraid that you might get sick, so when I went to bed at night, I always prayed, 'God, please, don't let anything happen to my mother'." Füsun covered her face with her hands and stayed like that for a while. Then she lowered his hands, looked at his son's face, and continued:

"When your father and I got divorced, I couldn't accept it at first. I have inflicted so much pain on myself and on you, I couldn't help it." Yiğit said, "Back then, I was not sad because my father had gone, but because you were so sad and crying." Füsun said,

"But I realized that much later. I was too late to realize that my unhappiness and my difficulty in accepting what happened was only hurting you."

"I can't say it didn't do any harm," Yiğit said, slowly shaking his head from side to side. "I know I caused a lot of damage.

Both to you and Zeynep," said Füsun. Yiğit said, "Don't forget the damage you caused to yourself."

"You know, I blamed your father a lot in the beginning; yes, but I was guilty at least as he was by putting this event at the center of my life, or rather our lives," said Füsun, as if confessing.

"Your father had decided to take that direction in his life, and he did it. In his advice to you, he would always say, 'Decide your own direction and do whatever it takes to go in that direction, the most important thing is your happiness'. I guess we were a little late in deciding our direction after the divorce."

"A little?" said Yiğit. Füsun began to cry again. Yiğit got up and sat next to his mother, hugging her neck. Füsun couldn't help crying even more; she put her head on her son's chest, and said,

"I'm sorry for all those days, hours, and years that I left you alone because of my anger, for leaving you without me. I love you so, so much." While Yiğit was stroking his mother's hair, Füsun continued:

"We can start all over again, please give us a chance," said Füsun, wiping her nose with the handkerchief in her hand. In the meantime, she lifted her head and started to look at her son's face.

"What do you mean another chance?" asked Yiğit, looking at his mother with questioning eyes.

"Please accept to get treatment," said Füsun, looking at her son with pleading eyes. Yiğit remained silent for a while; he thought with his eyes looking forward. For a while they were both silent. Finally, Yiğit said;

"I love you so much that I can't stand your being sad. I will get treated for your sake," he said.

"But just for your sake," he added.

"You may have forgiven my father, but it may take a little longer for me," he said as he pressed her mother's head into his chest.

When Yiğit accepted to be treated, Füsun immediately called her son Cem to share the good news and asked him to inform his father. When Cem, who was working as an assistant at the university hospital and tried to support his family as much as he could despite being very busy with work, called his father, Emin said,

"Tell your mother not to worry, I will do whatever is necessary."

As a result of their research, Emin and Cem learned that the psychiatric hospital in Manisa was one of the best hospitals in addiction treatment, so they chose that hospital for Yiğit's treatment. Because the demand for the hospital was so high, they had to wait for a while. During this time, Emin had to talk to the hospital many times, discussing the conditions, planning the hospitalization date, and waiting for a private room. According to their plans, Emin would come to Adana from Izmir by plane and take Yiğit to Manisa by a car he would rent.

When the deadline for hospitalization finally arrived, they were all in a hurry. A few hours before the admission, Füsun was preparing Yiğit's suitcase on the one hand, and on the other hand, she was occasionally going to her room to secretly cry, suppressing her sobs so that her son would not hear her crying: 'What would her baby boy do there all by himself?', 'Would he suffer a lot?', 'Was it a good idea to send him so far?' she was thinking. She was trying hard to be strong, but there was no way to relieve the pain in her chest.

Füsun had spent the whole night with so many thoughts in her head without getting a wink of sleep until the morning. She didn't want to be in the same car with Emin, so she sent them alone, but she was planning to visit her son as soon as possible. When she told him this, Yiğit said,

"There is no need for you to come, mother," even though he was feeling otherwise in his heart.

As they had agreed the night before, Yiğit and Emin set off from Adana early on a cold winter morning. Cem was with Füsun in the early morning when they were saying goodbye, as Füsun poured a bowl of water on the road behind the car as they left, saying 'Let the time flow by like water.'

On the way, Emin's attempts at starting a conversation were left unanswered by Yiğit. Yiğit was almost withdrawn into his own world; he was quiet and thoughtful. He gave short answers to Emin's questions, remained indifferent to the things he said, not saying a word in return. So many thoughts were running through his head about why he was there, cursing the day he was born.

Realizing that he was rowing against the tide, Emin lapsed into silence after a while as well. The ride was interrupted only by a few breaks and it continued without speaking except for when it was necessary. They were both withdrawn into their own worlds, only accompanied by the radio and cassette player.

It was getting dark when they reached Manisa and entered through the garden of the hospital. As they got out of the car in the parking lot, icy cold air hit their faces. When Yiğit saw the yellow walls of the hospital, looking colder than the air, he already regretted coming. They walked together towards the hospital. They barely talked during the admission procedures except when it was necessary. Emin had to go out and get a few things the hospital asked for. After getting them, he accommodated his son in his room, stayed with him for a while, and he hugged him tightly before leaving, finding it hard to let him go. When he finally did and looked at his face, he saw that there were tears in Yiğit's eyes, increasing his sadness tenfold.

Getting into the car at midnight to return to Izmir, Emin realized that high walls had been built between him and his younger son for years. Each day they were apart added a brick on the wall between them. It shattered his heart that his son didn't trust him, that he thought he never loved him, and that he was now leaving him there alone. While he was on his way to İzmir, he could not bear the weight of these thoughts that came over him like a nightmare, and holding the steering wheel tightly, with his eyes on the road, he cried and cried, screaming and slobbering...

DESPITE EVERYTHING, THERE IS ALWAYS HOPE

37) YİĞİT'S TRAVEL TO ENGLAND... 1995

After the treatment at the hospital, Yiğit was finally free of drug addiction and he was discharged after two months. Füsun, who went to visit him several times, realized each time that her son was better than her previous visit. It was a relief to see his progress.

After leaving the hospital, there were also changes in the relationship between mother and son; their bond became even stronger. This period was very nice for Füsun, she would look into Yiğit's eyes and do whatever it took to make him happy. Füsun thought that she and Emin should plan for his future. They had no idea what to do, but they had to wait a bit. The boy needed a little rest to collect himself, to get away a little from this miserable life he had.

One evening while they were watching a game on TV, Yiğit, with his eyes on the screen, said,

"This is probably the place I want to see the most in the world," as if talking to himself. Füsun, who heard him, could not understand what the place was, and asked,

"Where is that," asked him to repeat it, and she kept the name of the place in her mind, which she heard of for the first time in her life. Füsun had been thinking for a while that her son had gone through a lot of hardship, he had accomplished something amazing, and he needed a trip. So why not go to this place, she thought.

The next day she called Emin and told him about her plan. He, too, thought that it was a good idea, told her not to worry about money at all, and said that he would finance all their travel expenses. Just as he was hanging up the phone, he had thanked Füsun for thinking and undertaking such a thing.

Yiğit thought his mother was joking when he heard that they were going to England to see the Old Trafford stadium in Manchester. The idea excited him and made him happier than he had been in a long time. He later admitted that until the flight, he feared that his mother might be afraid of flying and give up at the last minute.

This trip abroad was very good for both of them. Mother and son had a great time. When they returned home at the end of a week, both of them felt refreshed and looked to the future with more hope.

SOMETIMES, YOU FEEL HELPLESS IN LIFE

38) YİĞİT GETS A JOB AT FOOTBALL PITCH... 1995

Shortly after the vacation, Yiğit started working at a football pitch, a job his uncle arranged for him. His job was to plan the schedules of the games, to deal with the pitch, to send jerseys to the laundry, to deal with the customers, all of which he enjoyed doing.

Kadir, whose nickname was 'Baba' and who was a friend of his father, knew about Yiğit's past and what he had been through and he liked Yiğit a lot; his hard work, decency, and honesty impressed him. He was doing his job thoroughly, solving problems with his agile mind, and adding value to the business by going beyond expectations. He was always coming up with new things that made Kadir Baba say,

“Wow, why didn't I think of this before?”. Things were running smoother than ever before. The number of customers had increased, the demand was so high that they had to give appointments for future dates to their customers.

Yiğit worked there for about two years, he was running the place together with Kadir Baba, who even let him run the cash register with peace of mind. That lasted until the group of old friends that he hadn't seen for a long time and didn't want to see came to the pitch to play a match one day. The group of hoodlums, consisting of seven or eight men who instantly recognized Yiğit, surrounded his table after their match. They influenced Yiğit, who was no longer interested in those things and even arranged the place where they wanted him to come. He could not resist the insistence of this group, who said that they would just chat for the sake of the old days, that they missed him very much, that they wanted to get together with him in honor of Mustafa, who was now in prison.

"Okay, I'll be there at seven o'clock tomorrow night," he said. Kadir Baba was not there that day. If he was, perhaps he would stop him, begging him not to go to that meeting that would have cost him his life.

Adana was not a very big city. It was not easy to avoid things, trouble would somehow come and find one. Once in that environment, the rest happened quickly and he was involved once again with that evil thing. Once again, it started little by little, tolerance developed after a while, he increased the dose again and had to find a stronger substance as that one no longer had the expected effect. The whole cycle was repeated, but all these happened much faster because his body was already familiar with the substances. He was a drug addict again, with needs that were very difficult to satisfy, and these substances were not meeting his emotional needs, but they were rather intensifying them even more.

Yiğit started to find it difficult to do things he used to enjoy doing because he couldn't keep his mind together. He was mixing accounts, arguing with customers, overreacting to events. At first, Kadir Baba could not understand what was happening, but soon he realized the situation and he felt a deep pain in his heart. It was very clear that Yiğit was not his previous self anymore; it was apparent from the way he looked and carried himself. Kadir Baba tried very hard to get Yiğit back, whom he loved like a son. He made him make a lot of promises, knowing that he could not keep them, he talked to a lot of people, but in the end, he did not succeed. Because he was sick of his advice and annoyed with the pain in the neck called Kadir - these were Yiğit's words - he decided to quit his job and he did not go back after that decision.

Kadir Baba was devastated, he called Emin, thinking that it was his duty to let him know. While telling him that Yiğit was not coming to work anymore, that he could not take care of him, that he slipped out of his hands, and that he couldn't do anything, he asked him to forgive him and burst into tears. When Emin called Füsun, she said with pain that she had guessed this and suspected it for a long time.

LIFE MAY SHAKE YOU AT A TIME YOU NEVER EXPECTED

39) FÜSUN IS DESTROYED BY WHAT SHE HEARS... 1995

Pelin, who was already unhappy because she was in Adana and did not like her mother-in-law and Yiğit, kept talking about this all the time, making Cem very sad. In the early stages of his specialization training, Cem worked shifts very often and spent very little time at home. Even during the limited time he was at home, Pelin's reproaches did not seem to end. According to her, Cem was spending too much energy to solve Yiğit's problems on top of working a lot and getting tired at the hospital. She thought that her husband was spending the time he should spend for herself for his own siblings and mother.

Füsun, on the other hand, always valued Pelin, thinking that 'if her son loves her, she is worth being loved', and always tried to think positively about her. She was attributing her mistakes to her youth; she believed they would diminish as she got more mature. Zeynep thought Pelin was selfish and narcissistic, and she did not like her very much either. Whenever she came up during a conversation, she would angrily say,

"I put up with this woman for my brother's sake." Füsun sometimes had to keep Zeynep from fighting with Pelin. No matter how hard she tried, there were inevitable quarrels between them.

Tuna was born two years after Cem and Pelin moved to Adana. Füsun was devastated by an event she went through after the birth of her grandson, which she later wished hadn't happened;

Pelin's mother, father, and sister came from Istanbul when she gave birth to Tuna, which brought joy to both sides of the family. It was the first time they had been to their daughter's house since the wedding three years ago. Füsun was very happy to hear that they had come and believed that she should be there, wanted to be there to see both Pelin's family and her grandson, and went to her son and daughter-in-law's house.

After eating the lunch consisting of lahmacun and Adana kebab that Cem ordered, Cem went out with his father-in-law and the women stayed at home. Füsun felt tired after having a little chat and drinking tea, asked permission, and went to the other room to get a little rest. At that time, Füsun was enjoying her retirement. Although she never shared this with her children, or even tried to keep it secret, she realized that she was getting tired very quickly lately and from time to time, she had difficulty breathing. Of course, at that time, no one could have guessed that she had a relentless disease and that her fatigue was one of the first symptoms of this illness.

She had fallen asleep where she lay to rest; she didn't realize how much time had passed, but when she opened her eyes, she felt rested. She opened the door and stepped out into the hallway when she heard her name and paused. It was as if Pelin and her family were talking about her. Pelin was saying,

"I hate that crazy woman," probably referring to Zeynep. Her elder sister said,

"The whole family is crazy, their son is a drug addict too,

they don't even know where he is." Her mother said,

"That's just your luck, my daughter," in a tearful voice. Her elder sister said,

"Only Cem seems to be normal in the whole family," Pelin said,

"His father felt what was going to happen when Cem was little, so he left them and ran away with another woman and settled in Izmir." Her mother said,

"The poor guy must have felt beforehand what would happen," and they all burst into laughter.

"Oh, my poor daughter..." her mother was saying. Pelin said,

"Well, Mrs. Füsun took a lot of antidepressants in the past too, tranquilizers and stuff like that...." Füsun was stunned. She couldn't believe her ears. They were basically judging all of them one by one. She suddenly felt nauseous. She intended to get over her shock and go back to the room she came from when she came face to face with Pelin who came to the hallway. From the expression on Füsun's face, Pelin understood that she heard what they were talking about. Now it was her turn to be stunned, and all she could say with a barely audible voice was,

"Come, mother, we were drinking coffee."

"I'll leave, you can drink your coffee," she said. She didn't even want to go to the living room to say goodbye, she just hastily left in anger. She was very upset, she thought she didn't deserve any of this and felt angry with Pelin and her family. Her anger did not mitigate on the way home or when she arrived home. Despite Zeynep's persistent questions to find out what happened, who saw her mother was silent and pensive all night long and felt that this was not normal, she did not open her mouth and say a word about it. This would have made Zeynep even more aggressive towards Pelin. She could never guess what

Zeynep might do, she might go there and yell at them, burning all bridges, which might cause an irreversible situation between them. That was totally unnecessary.

In fact, she knew that Pelin had a bad relationship with her mother and sister until she got married, she knew that she especially hated her mother. She remembered that Cem had once mentioned something like that about Pelin and her family. It seems like a lot of things changed after the marriage.

That even really shook Füsun. Over time, she got over this experience, did not tell anyone about this incident, always kept it a secret, but her heart would be broken over this for a long time... Pelin, on the other hand, felt ashamed as she looked at her face, but she had never thought of asking Füsun's forgiveness or talking about it. Up until that evening of disaster that would cause Füsun a lot of pain and suffering...

As Tuna grew up, Pelin would begin to think that her husband neglected her son Tuna this time because of his family, and she would keep finding reasons to start new fights.

ADDICTION MAKES INTELLIGENCE AND WILLPOWER UNFUNCTIONAL.

40) YİĞİT STARTS TO WORK WITH ZEYNEP... 1997

After Yiğit quit his job at the football pitch, he worked couple more jobs that his brother and mother arranged, but could not keep any of them. Those who found out that he was an addict did not give him a job. Using drugs prevented him from participating in social life and establishing normal relationships with people. As the drugs were running through his veins, he didn't seem concerned about anything and felt more powerful, able to overcome anything in life. When the effects of the substances would end and he would return to normal, he would want more, keeping him in a loop of searching for more, finding it, and taking it again. The effort, money, and time it took to get more had become indispensable in this vicious cycle of life.

In fact, Yiğit was a very good person; he would make every sacrifice for his loved ones, and if they were in trouble, he would run to their help no matter what. Even though his friends did him wrong many times, he still didn't stop believing them. Although he promised himself that he would be smarter after each incident, he would still make the same mistakes in a similar situation. In the family, his problem was with his elder sister Zeynep; his mother, on the other hand, was precious to him, he would never want her to feel sad.

The assistant boy at Zeynep's painting workshop who ran errands and kept records had made Zeynep very angry once because he had made a wrong shipment. Three days ago, when he was late in receiving orders from Zeynep, she had given him a strong scolding and then dismissed him. In fact, it was a time when orders were piling up and customers were getting angry, so she should not have fired him at all. Zeynep's character, who didn't care about anything when she was angry, was also a known fact. At that time, when it was difficult for her to keep up with everything and she felt helpless because she could not find a new assistant, she said to her brother:

"You can come and help me if you wish until you find something new." Yiğit had looked calmer for some time and he was spending most nights at home, he also seemed calmer towards Zeynep and his mother. They had thought that he was matured now. But they didn't even think that the reason for this might be a woman in Yiğit's life who made him feel that she was there for him, who allowed him to hold her hand and made him happy.

Asuman was the sister of a boy named Ozan, one of Yiğit's friends, he stayed at his place from time to time when he didn't go back home - they would later become roommates. He used to meet Ozan when he was working at the football pitch, and they continued their friendship later on. One day, he saw Asuman by chance when she brought food to her brother's house when he was there. He liked her very much the moment he saw her.

She was a cheerful girl and warmly looked at Yiğit with her big black eyes. She spoke slowly, and it was evident that she loved her brother very much. When she arrived, she prepared the dinner table, added oil and lemon to the salad she brought, cut the bread, put the food on the plates, and welcomed them to the table. While they were having their meal, she tidied up and organized the house. Later, they all drank the tea that Asuman brewed and ate the cookies she brought.

Ozan's father was a truck driver. He was an ignorant, indifferent, selfish person. He put too much pressure on his family. Since he did not care much about his children's education, it suited his book when Ozan left high school and began to work. Ozan got a job at an auto repair shop. Every month, he gave the money he earned to his mother, who was neglected by his father both financially and emotionally. Ozan could do anything for his mother and sister; when his father went on a long-distance drive for his job, he took care of his mother and sister.

One day, Ozan disagreed with his father about something. Because he thought he was right, he did not budge about the issue. His father, who thought that he was wrong in standing up to him, kicked him out of the house without hesitation. He didn't care what he would do or where he would go. First, he started sleeping at the auto repair shop where he worked; when winter came and this was not possible, he rented a broken-down place with a friend for a cheap price.

It was where Yiğit met Asuman. After seeing her, he began to visit Ozan more frequently. Sometimes, when he brought kebab wrap or lahmacun and went to his place, he would hope that Asuman was there too. Asuman liked him too, and she could always find an excuse to tell her mother to visit her brother Ozan. Thus, they began to meet outside without telling Ozan. Yiğit was in love; his life became somewhat more arranged, and he had not been this happy for a long time. When he saw Asuman, he could not prevent his heart from beating faster, and when they were in the same room, he would get very excited.

Zeynep made the offer to work together at the workshop while Yiğit felt above the clouds and had hope for the future:

"Let me think about it a little," Yiğit told her.

He was actually thinking whether it would be a problem to be in the same place with Zeynep, who was a very difficult person to deal with.

"You find a job and you're going to think about it?" Zeynep grumbled angrily. Then she made a joke, saying,

"The job you will do is very easy, and I will even give you a salary."

Thus, Yiğit began to go to Zeynep's workshop. He kept the book of the workshop, took orders, informed customers politely, took care of the shipments, and organized the courses Zeynep gave. He even stayed there most nights, opening the workshop early in the morning, cleaning and ventilating it until Zeynep arrived. Moreover, thanks to Yiğit, they began to deliver orders much faster, and they started to run the workshop more smoothly. Füsun was very happy to see that Zeynep was supporting her brother and that the arguments, conflicts, and insults they had in the past had decreased.

Yiğit successfully completed each task he was given, fulfilling his responsibilities in the best way possible. Just as he had done miracles working with Kadir Baba at the football pitch when he was clean; it was certain that he would have been very successful in life if he hadn't been involved with drugs before.

But this period of felicity would not last long. About seven months after beginning this job, Asuman's father, who somehow found out that his daughter met Yiğit, got very angry and forbade her to go out. Afterward, he could not control his anger and sent her to their village, ignoring the pleas of Asuman and her mother. Yiğit was worried when Asuman did not show up at the place where they agreed to meet, and when he asked Ozan, he found out that Asuman was sent to the village. And that she could not come back to Adana until her father would let her...

After hearing what had happened, nothing mattered to Yiğit anymore, the entire world came crashing about his ears. How happy he had been for months. It was a severe blow for Yiğit, and he almost fell into depression, he started to neglect his work at the workshop from time to time. Again, he was going through a phase where he had no more hope left and the future seemed very grim. He felt the heavy weight of the life on his shoulders again.

He was not fulfilling his responsibilities anymore, which he had done with pleasure in the past. When Zeynep would arrive late in the morning, she would find Yiğit still sleeping in the bed and the workshop in a mess. This made Zeynep very angry. At first she politely warned her brother several times. But she was getting angry and starting to grumble as long as Yiğit didn't get his act together despite all her warnings. Yiğit's latest incident was the last straw that ruined the relationship between them, which was already hanging by the eyelids.

On a cold December evening, Yiğit invited a friend over to the workshop when asked for help because he did not have a place to stay for the night. The night that started with him and his friend, continued with four people as two more of their friends came over as well. On that night, when it was cold and stormy outside, they had taken alcohol and drugs in the workshop warmed by the heater, laying down on the seats and cushions, and ended the night there with the wind howling outside. When Zeynep came to the workshop in the morning and saw that the place was a mess, she was mad with anger. The bad odor, the liquor bottles scattered all over the place, shattered glass pieces on the floor, nutshells all over the place, and alcohol spilled on the sofa and floor...

She shook Yiğit awake, said whatever came to her mind and insulted him.

"I don't know how you managed to be so amenable for a long time without numbing yourself anyway. So you had been pretending," said Zeynep, shouting in anger. She had Yiğit and his three friends, who were all unconscious and very difficult to sober up, get out of there by calling the police. The police had gathered them all in the police car and took them to the police station to take their testimonies.

Zeynep would then go even further, claiming that Yiğit stole some of the money she hid in the workshop. It was no use for Yiğit to say he did not do such a thing. When the truth came out, it would be too late to do something... Füsun felt she aged a few years with each incident regarding Yiğit, and she was very worn by these latest events. She of course did not approve of what her son did, but what her daughter did was incomprehensible as well.

After Zeynep had them kicked out of the workshop that night, Yiğit did not show up for a long time; Füsun's and Cem's efforts to reach him had also failed. Füsun had waited for her son for days with her eyes on the street, hoping for his return. As a matter of fact, Yiğit came back when he felt like seeing his mother. He spent time with his mother, told her he could not stay in that house with Zeynep any longer, and said,

"Otherwise, I might do things I will regret," leaving Füsun nothing to say.

When he came home to see his mother, he carefully chose the times when Zeynep was not home. He didn't want to see her, he usually spent the night elsewhere, and he didn't reveal anything about where he was staying. As a result of the incidents Yiğit was involved in, Füsun was called to the police station several times, and she had to spend very bad days and nights.

Füsun, together with Cem, convinced Yiğit once again that he should be treated, even though it was difficult. This time, he received inpatient treatment at Adana Mental Health Hospital. After being discharged from the hospital, Yiğit could stay clean for a much shorter time, and he started taking drugs again after eight months. It became evident that Yiğit could no longer return to normal with treatments, and he would live the rest of his life as a lost soul, until that disastrous day...

PERSONALITY IS THE MOST IMPORTANT FACTOR DETERMINING OUR BEHAVIOR

41) YİĞİT GETS BEATEN… 1998

Yiğit was now among houses leaning against each other, in secluded corners and dark narrow neighborhoods. He was wandering around neighborhoods with tightly closed curtains, where it was not clear whether people lived or not. He had to go to those places to find drugs. His days felt like dreams haphazardly passing by, so he had no concern about his future anymore.

One evening, he had to go to one of those neighborhoods again, he had taken drugs for a few days and was walking absent-mindedly. He saw a man, whose white shirt turned gray with dirt, with his beard and hair tangled, whose age he could not guess, beating a child around the age of eight or nine with his belt. The boy was crouched down with his tiny body, trying to protect his head. Yiğit didn't care how stupid or brave what he was about to do was, and he yelled at the man,

"Hey what are you doing?". He didn't know yet that it was

their turf and they called the shots there.

"It is not your business!" growled the man.

"What could such a small child have done to be beaten up so badly?" said Yiğit. The man grinned,

"I can give you half of the beating that is his right if it bothers you so much," walking towards Yiğit and swinging the belt in his hand towards him. As Yiğit stepped backward just in time, the belt whipped the air without touching him. The man got very angry when he swung the belt and missed Yiğit for a second time, and he roared,

"Come here!". Just as Yiğit realized that he needed to make a run for it and was getting ready to do it, another man came out of one of the run-down houses, and said,

"I think you need help, Hilmi," laughing and making a move towards Yiğit, grabbing his arms from behind. The man called Hilmi, who threw the belt in his hand to the ground, took a few steps towards them, he said,

"Let's teach you a lesson, you bastard," and punched Yiğit in the face with all his might. Yiğit felt a severe pain in his jaw. The other man had let go of his arms, and he had started hitting Yiğit as well. Although Yiğit tried to resist, to punch them – he was able to hit them a few times too – he could not fight against their attacks. Yiğit, who was beaten badly by these men, fell to the ground and remained there like a mess. He couldn't move, and it was now very difficult for him to resist their punches and kicks.

"Wait, what are you doing! Are you crazy?" Despite the voices shouting at them, the men continued to beat him. The person who shouted came running towards them, and said,

"What are you doing, Hilmi?" squatting down, stretching his hands over Yiğit, he yelled,

"Don't do it! Stop!" he shouted. The two men seemed to come to their senses with that voice and they suddenly stopped.

"We showed this little boy what it means to poke his nose into other people's business," said Hilmi.

"You made a mistake, he is from us, Mustafa entrusted him to us," the man said. Hilmi calmed down and growled,

"Abbas, take him out of here, I don't want to see him," and the man beside him followed as he turned his back and left.

Yiğit looked like a mess, his clothes were ripped, covered with dust, and he was on the ground. One of his eyes was badly swollen and bruised. His mouth and nose covered in blood, Abbas tried to lift him from the ground and said,

"What have you done, boy? You shouldn't mess with these types." He took him by the arm, lifted him from the ground with great difficulty, carried him by the wall, and made him sit on the ground, leaning his back against the wall. Drops of blood flowing from Yiğit's nose covered his lip and dripped onto his light yellow shirt. The man left him there for a little while, then came back with gauze and disinfectant and began to clean Yiğit's face. On the one hand, he was grumbling,

"Why would you mess with people you don't know?", "Why would you meddle in things that are none of your business, kid?", "You don't know about these places". Yiğit had recognized him; it was the man called Abbas, from whom he bought drugs. When Yiğit tried to say something, he silenced him, saying,

"Shut up, don't talk now." The man checked Yiğit's bleeding cuts and bones one by one, decided that it was not necessary for him to go to the hospital, he said,

"Wait here," and disappeared. After a while, Yiğit tried to get up, but he was not sure that he could stand on his feet. Still, he was thinking about what he could do, moving his hands and feet, watching his surroundings to find help when a car stopped in front of him. When the driver got out of the car and came towards him, he saw that it was Abbas who had just helped him. While trying to get Yiğit off the ground by coming up to him, he said

"Come on, boy, I'll drop you home." He seated Yiğit in the back of the car, a very old model, an almost broken down Murat 131 that felt like it was barely working. Everything hurt on Yiğit's body as he got in the car, but he didn't say anything since he was grateful, clenching his teeth and trying not to make a sound.

On the way, Abbas talked about Hilmi, who had beaten him. Since he was making money off of children; "Children bring money, he spends it," he said.

It seemed to Yiğit that there was hostility between them. God knows what the issue was between them. This was the last thing Yiğit wondered about right now. He couldn't help thinking about why the man had helped him. Maybe he wanted to find out where he lived by taking him home or maybe he just wanted to help. Of course, it was impossible to find out now.

"You seem like a good boy," Abbas said.

"We don't like doing this job either but we need to keep food on the table too," he said. Looking at Yiğit in the backseat on the rear view mirror.

"There are rules in this business, like every other business, and I'm against using kids in this business," he said, who had just sold him drugs a little earlier.

"Hilmi has children, each work in a different way and bring him money. Some sell handkerchiefs, some beg, some weigh people with scales." While listening to Abbas, Yiğit thought about the phrase 'no one can be trusted in this business', which he heard very often from many people.

"Do you know why he was beating that boy?" he asked, looking at him on the mirror. Yiğit was also wondering about this, so he listened to Abbas looking at his eyes on the rearview mirror.

According to what he said, this kid was weighing people with a scale every day on a sidewalk, and this time they put a broken scale and a stone large enough to fit in a palm in front of this kid. When soft-hearted people would ask what happened, seeing the kid crying and the broken scale, he was supposed to say 'three older boys came, threw the stone on his scale, and broke it.' Upon hearing this, the kind-hearted people -mostly women- were giving him enough money to buy a new scale. In fact, there were times when three or five people were collecting money from each other and giving the crying kid a higher amount of money.

"That's how they exploit emotions," said Abbas. Yiğit was shocked by what he heard.

"The crime of that boy was that someone saw him taking the broken scale and the stone out of his sack and reported him to the police," said Abbas.

"They took the boy to the police station and took his statement. Luckily, he said that he planned it all, so they gave him some advice and released him," said Abbas.

Yiğit had him drop him off at a friend's house, where he stayed from time to time. Füsun would see his face a few days later when he visited and she would be very sad. His mother, who would be shocked if she learned how the incident happened, would not learn anything from Yiğit despite her insistence.

A SUFFERING FAMILY MEMBER BRINGS THE FAMILY TOGETHER

42) THEY FIND OUT THAT FÜSUN HAS AN ILLNESS... 1998

Füsun was fifty-six years old when she was diagnosed with lung cancer. The news of the disease afflicted the whole family and shocked everyone. The treatment was started immediately after diagnosis. Treatment protocols with varying duration, types, and amounts were applied at various times, and she had to receive either chemotherapy or radiotherapy at different times. Her life quality changed depending on the treatment she received at the moment; there were times when she felt extremely tired and slept all day long. Füsun suffered a lot. She had rashes on her body, sores in her mouth, she suffered hair loss, and there were periods when she vomited excessively. This process was very painful for the whole family, and everyone did their best to support her.

After the doctors said that there was no chance of recovery, Cem, Zeynep, and even Yiğit began to spend more time with her, doing anything she wanted. Now that she needed constant care during the day, and she couldn't be alone,she was with a daycare assistant, whom Cem found after a lot of effort. She had to receive psychological support too as she experienced periods of intense depression from time to time. As a physician, she saw that she had no choice but to accept certain things; she prayed profusely.

Zeynep, who was twenty-seven years old when her mother was diagnosed with cancer, felt better when she took her medications regularly, and her tolerance for daily life increased. She had matured and had a better understanding of her mother. Sometimes, when she thought about the past, she remembered what she had done to her mother and felt a deep pain in her heart. Because she wanted to spend more time with her, she would close her workshop and come home early. They were having conversations more frequently than ever. Füsun didn't have much time left, and these conversations were Zeynep's last chance to hear some of the stories her mother would take with her. Zeynep was sometimes taking her glass of red wine, which she liked to drink after dinner, and sitting on the floor in front of her mother's armchair, starting a conversation by asking,

“Do you remember mom?”. She liked to talk about the past by looking into her eyes, to learn how her mother felt at that time, to listen to the reasons for her behavior back then.

It was at that time she realized that many things did not happen as she thought.

One night, they were talking about her friend Doğa. Zeynep talked about how they moved to Bursa in the middle of the school year and that they called each other very often at first, but their calls became infrequent over time. She reminded her mother that her friend meant a lot to her at the time, that she wanted to buy her a gift, but she refused to go shopping with her, saying 'I have a meeting'. Füsun said,

“I remember that incident,” fixing her eyes on a distant spot. She explained Zeynep how that week was maybe the worst period in her life, how she had a problem with a colleague, and she had an appointment with her psychiatrist that Saturday, which she was afraid to tell Zeynep about for some reason.

"So I wasn't in a mood to go shopping," she added. Hearing these, Zeynep said,

"But I thought…" with a sad voice. Füsun confessed that she did not realize how important her friend was for her at that time, she was unfortunately too busy with her own problems, and she knew then what she knows now, she would have gladly gone shopping with her, and added,

"I'm sorry for that day." Zeynep, looking at her lovingly, reached forward and pushed her mother's hair back with her fingers. Füsun's hair had been white for a long time, there were sparse and thin strands on her head that grew after she lost her hair during chemotherapy.

"Don't apologize because I gave the golden necklace you bought me for my birthday as a gift to Doğa," she said with a smile, her eyes were full of tears…

Yiğit, who came to the house from time to time, was fussing over his mother as well. It pained Füsun to accept the fact that there was not much anyone could do about his drug addiction, that people around him had to accept it and that he would live that way now.

Yiğit was living with his friend Ozan in a house that Cem bought when he came to Adana. However, Füsun could not neglect him, she would tell him to come over whenever she could cook and Yiğit would either come over and eat there or take the food with him to his place to eat with his friend.

Yiğit couldn't keep up with the jobs he started. He would go in and work for a while, then he would cause a scene and never go back. He was a very energetic, well-spoken, popular person under the influence of drugs. But during drug withdrawal, he would be extremely angry and aggressive. At such moments, he would often start a fight, shouting or beating people, depending on the person he was dealing with, or he was getting beaten. When he was beaten, he would stay at home because of the cuts and bruises on his face, and he did not want his mother to see him like that. When it was necessary to reach Yiğit's family, Zeynep was directly calling Cem and he was taking care of Yiğit now since it was hard for Füsun to take care of him now. Even though he knew that his wife did not like this situation at all, Cem would go without hesitation, either getting him out of custody or picking him up from the hospital.

Füsun, who thought that Cem had a family and a son who needed his father, was trying to keep him away from her own problems, and she wouldn't call him unless she had to. She was trying to solve her problems with the daycare assistant woman who stayed with her at home. It was also during this period that she started to tell white lies to Cem to make sure that he was with his family.

But she was getting increasingly worried about Yiğit's future, and she was wondering what would happen to him when she was not there anymore. For that reason, she asked Cem to come over one day,

"Look, this is my will, Cem," she began speaking.

To Cem, who said, "What kind of word is that, mother...":

she replied, "We are both physicians and we both know more or less what will happen to me." Now, they were both silent, waiting. At the end of a long silence, when Füsun finally spoke, she said,

"Look son, all I'm asking you is to take care of your brother."

"Mom, of course, we won't leave our brother alone, don't worry," replied Cem. Although he was very worried about Yiğit's future as well, he thought that there was no point in sharing this with his mother at the moment.

"I want to leave all my possessions to him and I'm asking for your forgiveness for this. I will ask Zeynep the same thing," said Füsun.

"Of course, mom, you don't even have to say it," said Cem.

"Do you know? I have always been afraid that one day I would find out that Yiğit died of an overdose, but as you can see, life is full of surprises."

"Unfortunately, mom, we never know what awaits us," said Cem.

Füsun's eyes filled with tears when she said, "Please, treatment or drug money, whatever is needed, use the money I will leave." Cem, who had never expected such a speech, also had tears in his eyes and was very confused.

Cem replied, "Don't worry mom, I'll do my best," but he didn't even have the slightest idea what he could do at that time...

As the years passed, people realize the importance of being a sibling, mother, or child, and the order of importance given to experiences and feelings may change.

IF YOU ARE WEAK, LIFE WILL CRUSH YOU WITHOUT MERCY

43) BACK WHEN LITTLE YİĞİT WAS GROWING UP...

Yiğit, who was always a quiet, calm, trouble-free child when he was little, was four when his parents got divorced. As far as he could understand with his little mind and from what he heard, his father had left and Yiğit was left with his mother and sister. Until he was old enough to know what marriage meant, he thought that it was normal for parents to live in separate houses. For that reason, one day, as his mother was putting his coat on, he asked his friend,

"Are you going to your mom or dad?". When Füsun heard this, her eyes filled with tears and she looked at Yiğit with pain. When he got a little older, he began to ask,

"Is Izmir more beautiful than Adana? Is that why my father lives there?". Füsun didn't know how to explain it.

All she could come up with was, "Your father found a better job there." She gave evasive answers to Yiğit's questions such as,

"Will he have more money now?", "Will he come back here when his job is done there?".

Yiğit was confused until he was able to understand some things about life, but at first, his childish thought was 'his father liked Izmir better so he went there and started to live with Alya's family.'

One day, he was happily walking beside his mother after kindergarten, reaching out to grab her hand, and bouncing on the street with his hand securely held by his mother. He was even singing a song he learned that day. Suddenly he heard his mother's voice coming from somewhere behind him. When he looked up at the person holding his hand, he saw that it was not his mother, and he immediately let go of her hand. At that moment, he thought that Elif's mother, whose hand he mistakenly held, was trying to kidnap him. He was so scared that he remembered his heart pounding like crazy as he let go of her hand and ran towards his mother. How did Elif's mother know about the conflict he had with Elif that day? he wondered, unable to come up with a logical reason with his child's mind. In this incident, where his trust in his mother was shaken, he could not understand why she only laughed when she saw what happened and did nothing when he was so afraid. For some reason, Yiğit never forgot about this incident with his mother from his childhood, which left a deep mark on his soul. Zeynep knew about this because Yiğit had told her, and when she told her mother about it, Füsun said that she could not remember that day.

While being separated from his father when he was little is a wound in itself, Yiğit also got used to things that had happened as he grew up, and he had to accept living like this as he got old enough to understand things. He even loved his father's house in Urla more than his own home in Adana at that time. The house had a huge pool and a big garden full of trees and flowers. It was very enjoyable to step into the porch from the exterior door, and then step into the garden from the porch, walking barefoot on the grass. He was always in the garden and he could do whatever he wanted, he would swim in the pool, paint, play hide-and-seek or house with Dila; he lived his days there to the fullest. He felt close to Dila, and he missed her when he went back to Adana until he saw her the next year.

Yiğit also loved the breakfasts they had out, all of them piling into the car. Everyone was very cheerful during these breakfasts. The place where they joyfully went was 'Ice Cream Maker Ali', where he was allowed to eat as much ice cream as he wanted. Yiğit's mother, who thought that he got sick very often, would never let him eat ice cream, but Aunt Gül did. Also, Aunt Gül was always smiling and tolerant, but he still couldn't behave whimsically towards her the way he did to his mother. For that reason, Yiğit would often think 'I wish my mother was here too'; there were especially some moments when he really wished she had been there with him.

When Yiğit was little, his sister's personality, rarely content and easily snapping in the face of negative events, affected him negatively. His little mind, whose reasoning ability was not yet fully developed, would be torn, not knowing what to think.

He remembered the day his father took them to the sea in Urla. Zeynep had put a damper on everything as always. He remembered how his older sister was very unhappy again, how she was not satisfied with anything, and how helpless his father was. They had hurriedly eaten in the cafeteria, after which his father had gone to buy them ice cream. Zeynep, staring at the shiny blue sea in front of them, had said,

"Alya, Dila, and their stupid mother took my father to Izmir." With his hat on his head and his cheeks red from the sun, Yiğit was quietly eating the french fries in front of him.

"Dad loves them more than us now," she continued. Yiğit raised his head and fixed his eyes on her, looking at her suspiciously. He thought, 'Could this be true?' Zeynep angrily said,

"That's why I hate them," starting to cry.

Yiğit believed what Zeynep said at that moment and became very upset. Even though an inner voice said that this was not possible, that Emin was only their father, that it was not possible for him to love those girls more, his childish mind could not deny the fact that she might be right. His elder sister was so unhappy that Yiğit remembered that he was also very sorry for her at that time.

When his father came back to the table with ice cream in his hand, he asked,

"What's going on, Zeynep?". Zeynep, who hadn't touched the food in front of her, looked at her father with tearful eyes and said,

"I want to go home," pushing the chair back, jumping up and heading for the door. Emin gave one of the ice creams to Yiğit, left the others in the food tray on the table, and followed Zeynep to the door, grumbling. Zeynep left her father's questions unanswered in the car, refusing to speak, and wept along the way.

When they returned home in the evening, she saw the doll in Dila's hand that her mother had bought for her that day. Dila got up and went to Emin, showed him her doll, and Emin kissed her on the cheek. While thinking about what his sister said during the day, Yiğit felt extreme jealousy and anger at that moment...

As he grew older, the most intense emotion in Yiğit's life would be loneliness. His father was always far away; he didn't even know him that well. They could see their father only in summers or occasionally when he came to Adana in between summers, and that was only for a few weeks. What his father did best was sending lots of money whenever he wanted.

When Cem returned to Adana for his residency training,

Yiğit had just finished high school and was very happy that his brother would now live in Adana. He loved and respected his brother, who always supported him financially and morally. He also went to his house several times to see his nephew. In his last visit, unfortunately, an unpleasant incident occurred with his brother, and this was the last time he visited him in his house.

That evening, when that unfortunate event happened, Cem, could not control his anger, who is normally a very calm person, and unpredictable things happened, Cem had invited his whole family to dinner.

Füsun had just been diagnosed with the disease. For Yiğit, who did not talk much even though he was in a family environment because he wasn't able to communicate well due to the drugs he took, things were very different when Tuna was in question. He loved his nephew very much, and when he saw him, it was as if he became a different person.

The dinner started and ended well. After dinner, they sat in the living room, sipping their tea. In one corner, Yiğit was holding Tuna on his lap, who was three years old at the time, asking him questions, and cheering up with the half-answers of the boy who was just starting to talk.

Pelin and Zeynep were talking about a newly opened department at Çukurova University, an initiative taken by an acquaintance of Pelin. They were talking about the foreign language education of the department. In the meantime, Cem went to the kitchen to get some tea for himself. Yiğit overheard the conversation going on and made a comment about the faculty. Pelin, who belittled him at every opportunity and did not hesitate to hurt his feelings, looked at him up and down and said,

"Wow! It is very tragicomic for you to make a comment like that as if you graduated from university." Angry at Pelin's comment, Zeynep said, "You don't need to graduate from university to know something." Pelin, on the other hand, continued,

"Still, a person should know his place in all circumstances and conditions. He shouldn't say big words when he is so small." Yiğit, who already had weak control over his anger due to his addiction, could not control himself when he heard those words. Leaving Tuna slowly on the ground, with fire in his eyes, he said,

"Look at me bitch!" grabbing Pelin's collar. At that time, Cem entered the room with his tea in his hand, and he was stunned by that sight, and said,

"What do you think you are doing?" grabbing Yiğit's arm and pulling him hard. This made Yiğit lose his balance, he hit one of the side tables and the table fell to the ground. Looking at his elder brother with fiery eyes, Yiğit swore a terrible obscenity at him. Hearing this, Cem couldn't control himself, he rushed forward and punched Yiğit in the jaw. Yiğit fell to the ground with this fist and as he tried to get up from the ground, Cem dragged him to the door and threw him out. Füsun and Zeynep were frozen and did not know what to do in this situation that happened within seconds.

Füsun was the first to get a grasp on herself when Yiğit was thrown out, and she was only able to shout,

"Cem what are you doing?". She dashed outside and helped Yiğit sit on one of the steps of the apartment stairs, telling him,

"Sit here, son, I'll be right back," she went back inside, collected her coat and purse without looking at any of them, and she went back to Yiğit. Meanwhile, Zeynep was putting on her shoes. After her mother walked out the door, Zeynep stared at Pelin, and said,

"Goddamn you," and headed for the stairs.

Yiğit never went back to his brother's house again. He did not speak to his wife unless he had to. Later on, Cem couldn't believe how he lost his temper and did something like this to his brother, and this would be the biggest regret of his life, always causing a twinge of conscience in him.

As he was trying to stay away from drugs and receive treatment, Yiğit's world came crashing down when he learned that his mother, the only person in the world whom he loved deeply and who supported him, had lung cancer. Around the same time, his girlfriend Asuman was sent to village by her father. The pain in his heart because of what happened to his loved one became unbearable after he learned about his mother's disease.

When he learned that his mother had cancer, Yiğit thought that life dealt him yet another blow. And it was the biggest blow yet. If she left too, there would be no one in the world to support him in life. It is a well-known fact that addicted people are unsuccessful in establishing and maintaining relationships. Unfortunately, there was not even a handful of people around Yiğit to support him.

He was already full of unhappiness and contradictions about himself, and he did not enjoy life much. Yiğit thought in this way at the time, he did not know that life didn't happen the way we plan it and it was full of unexpected surprises.

THE PERFECT FAVOR DOESN'T LEAVE ANYONE UNDER OBLIGATION TO RETURN IT

44) YİĞİT MEETS DİLA... 1998

"Hello, Dila, is that you? How are you?"

"I'm fine, I'm home, reading a book. How are you?"

"I need to see you."

"What happened, Yiğit? You don't sound good at all."

"I need to see you immediately."

"What happened, Yiğit, for God's sake?"

"Not on the phone, we have to meet."

"Okay," said Dila. They agreed to meet at the Mavi Köşe Patisserie an hour later. Dila tried to remember the last time she had seen her step-brother. It had been almost five years since they had graduated from high school.

When Dila entered through the door, she could not believe her eyes when she saw Yiğit sitting in a secluded corner of the patisserie. Yiğit was unrecognizable; he looked weak, his hair and beard were longer. He had rolled up the sleeves of his black sweater up to his elbows, revealing his tattoo design around his wrists. Everything was black: tattoos, sweater, jeans, boots… Dila couldn't tell if he had tinged his eyes with kohl or his eyelashes were darker. His face was pale, his eyes looked sunken, his lips looked purple. Dila was shocked, she slowly approached the table not taking her eyes off him, and sat down. The patisserie was dim and Yiğit looked tiny sitting across from her.

Dila didn't know how to begin, she was trying hard to blink her tears back. Yiğit was looking at her with a smile.

"Are you alright?" Dila asked slowly.

"I'm not bad," said Yiğit.

After the waiter who came to their table took their orders – they both ordered coffee-,

"How is your mother?" she asked this time.

"She is in the hospital, her condition is not good, she is suffering," Yiğit answered the question in a sad voice. Dila knew that Mrs. Füsun had cancer, so she said,

"I hope God will give her wellbeing." They were probably the picture of contradiction to the people looking from outside; a woman in a hijab and a man with fully black clothes, his arms covered in tattoos, his hair and beard long, his hands shaking.

The relationship between Yiğit and Dila, who always loved Yiğit and believed that he was a good person, was unlike any of the other siblings. These two step-siblings had always protected each other in high school and always kept in touch after high school, even if it was only on the phone. They always remembered each other's birthdays and called every year to celebrate. They loved each other like true siblings.

Dila was now remembering the summers they spent together in Urla and all the things they did together. She remembered how empty the house would become when they returned to Adana at the end of every summer. The image in her mind right now was how she cried for hours at the end of summer 'Because Yiğit was leaving'. They talked for a while about family members and what they were doing lately. She knew that Yiğit was not talking to Cem and they had not spoken for a long time.

Knowing that he needed support, Dila was sad to hear this. There was a short silence between them when Yiğit broke the silence by saying, "I was the one who tore off your doll's leg." "What?" Dila looked at him without understanding anything.

"You know, when you woke up in the morning at the house in Urla and your doll's leg was missing. I was the one who tore it off." Dila had to think about those childhood years for a moment to remember what he was talking about. They all had blamed Zeynep. Despite her denial, they were so sure that she had done it. She was very surprised, so she asked,

"Why did you do that?".

"Out of jealousy," Yiğit said with a laugh. Dila, who opened her eyes with curiosity, asked,

"Who were you jealous of, me?".

* BALZAC

"Zeynep had said that my father loved you more than us," he said. Dila didn't respond; she was immersed in the memories of those days, and she was thinking.

"You were so happy that I was obviously jealous of your happiness," said Yiğit. Dila silently looked at Yiğit and sighed deeply.

"I was little, I believed everything my sister said." Dila smiled,

"And we were so sure that Zeynep did it," she said, shaking her head slowly from side to side.

"I suddenly woke up at dawn in that morning. The emotions I felt at night were still there. You shouldn't have tried to take my father away from me. I was going to punish you. I came to your bedside and took your beautiful doll in a pink dress that you placed on the sofa before going to bed, and without giving it a thought, I tore off one of its legs in anger," he said. Dila's eyes were fixed on a spot on the table, she snapped back to reality with Yiğit's voice, who said,

"I realized what I had done when I found myself standing in your room with a leg in my hand." She looked at Yiğit's face for a few seconds, then burst into laughter. Yiğit, who looked at her with surprise at first, started to laugh as well. They both started laughing out loud. They couldn't stop themselves. When Dila realized that people sitting at the tables around them turned around and looked at them, she lowered her head down and continued to laugh for a while longer. Then, as she lifted her head, she reached for the napkin on the table to wipe tears from her eyes. Just when she was about the stop laughing, Yiğit said,

"I buried the leg next to the garden wall at the back," she burst into laughter again. She kept laughing for a while trying to be quiet with her head lowered, pressing the napkin on her lips.

When she lifted her head, this time, the tears she had been trying to blink back since she had arrived were starting to roll down her cheeks. Tears were falling one by one to her knees. The tears of joy had turned into tears of sadness. Yiğit was silently looking at his hands, his shaking hands.

"I haven't told anyone about this in fifteen years," he said in a low voice. After looking at Dila's face for a short time, Yiğit added,

"Seeing you sad and crying hurt me back then, but I just couldn't admit it, I was afraid," in a sad voice.

"We were just children and it was not possible for us to think like adults," said Dila as she wiped her tears.

"See, it's still bothering me because I felt the need to confess now, so I apologize even if it's too late," said Yiğit. Dila laughed and jokingly said,

"I accept your apology." For a while, they both sat in silence immersed in their own thoughts. Yiğit was looking in front of him, and Dila was looking out the window without seeing anything. Yiğit broke the silence and said,

"Dila, I need your help."

"I hope it's something I can do," said Dila.

"I need money," said Yiğit.

"How much?" asked Dila. When she heard the amount, she thought about her budget. She had some savings, but it was not enough for the amount Yiğit asked for. Perhaps she could ask her mother for the rest.

A voice in her head was telling her not to ask him why he needed that money because she wouldn't want to know. So she didn't ask.

The amount of money he asked for was not small, yes, but she knew that Yiğit wouldn't ask her if he didn't have to.

"You're not in trouble, are you, Yiğit?" Dila asked with fear in her heart.

"Don't worry, I'm not," he said. Dila was relieved upon hearing this.

"I think you shouldn't ask your mother for the money. My father may hear about it and I don't want him to know about it," said Yiğit. Dila nodded thoughtfully.

"Also, if he finds out, he will probably tell your mother not to give it," he said. After a short silence, Dila said,

"I'll find you this money, Yiğit, don't worry." Yiğit gratefully looked at Dila and said,

"Among the people I loved and trusted in my life, you are the only one who never let me down.”

“Likewise, I know I can always count on you,” Dila replied.

“Do you know? The bad days I am going through right now make me realize how good my days have been in the past,” said Yiğit sadly. Dila put her hand on Yiğit's hand on the table and said,

“May God always be with you brother. May God protect you and give you strength,” her eyes tearing up again. As they were saying goodbye, Dila said,

“I will find the money and bring it to you wherever you want.”

After leaving the patisserie, Dila was both crying and thinking while walking on the road. Yiğit's appearance, who had a bad fate in life, shook her and it took some time for her to get over it. She felt that Yiğit would find that money somehow, even if he had to steal. She did not have the heart to let him struggle to find it. She had to give him the money for the sake of the good times they had shared together.

“Sister, please don't ask me what I'm going to do with it, why I need it,” she said as she asked Alya for the remaining amount of money. Although Alya was curious, she did not insist and when she heard that everything was fine, she sent the money she wanted with peace of mind. She felt that the issue might be about Yiğit, but she just thought, 'I hope Dila knows what she is doing'.

After the disaster that befell Yiğit, Dila wondered for a long time if she had a share in it, even though she knew that it was impossible for her to find out...

IF YOU NUMB YOUR BRAIN, IT CAN HELP YOU

45) ZEYNEP KICKS OUT YİĞİT FROM THE EXHIBITION... 1999

Zeynep finally had the opportunity to have a 'painting exhibition', something she wanted to do for a long time but didn't have the opportunity. With the insistence of her friends and the support of Sinan, she would finally be able to exhibit her paintings with different subjects, styles, and genres at Çukurova Municipality Foyer Hall. Zeynep was very excited to share the paintings she had completed over the years with her loved one. Making the necessary agreements, arranging the organization company was all thanks to the efforts of Sinan, who supported her at all stages. A few days before the exhibition, Zeynep spent hours there and made all the arrangements so that everything could be perfect.

Finally, when the big day arrived, Zeynep looked beautiful with her light make-up, her loose ankle-length white dress, her white high heels, and tiny white flowers tied around her loosely pinned up hair. The opening was great, a faculty member gave a nice speech that cheered the audience. The flowers sent by the important people of Adana, who heard about the exhibition, were placed in the hall, the one sent by the mayor in the front. For a while, Zeynep's eyes were fixed on the flower sent by her father and Gül, making her smile happily. Her mother could not come because she had to go to the hospital for a treatment follow-up. But she had promised to stop by later if she felt better.

As the hours passed and the exhibition continued, the number of people did not decrease at all, and the ones who left were replaced with the ones who arrived. Conversations, music, cheerful laughter mixing in the cloud of sounds, and a clear word or sentence could be heard from time to time in the middle of all these sounds.

Zeynep was welcoming guests, champagne glass in her hand, and she was walking around small groups of people, chatting with them one by one. Almost everyone agreed that the paintings were magnificent. Zeynep was wandering among the guests, happy with their positive comments and congratulations. Sinan's presence gave strength to Zeynep, many people from his own social circle were at the exhibition as well. The guests were adapted to the environment, they were sipping their drinks and eating the small biscuits and cookies on the cocktail tables, having long conversations with each other.

Only fifteen minutes after Füsun arrived, having completed her routine checkup at the hospital, Yiğit showed up at the door. He was leaning on his friend standing next to him and looking more sober than him, he had trouble standing up as he was looking inside. Zeynep noticed them and immediately went over, fearing that Yiğit may cause a scene. Hissing through her teeth, she said,

"What are you doing here?" and tried to grab Yiğit by the arm to take him outside. He pulled his arm back strongly, saving himself from Zeynep's hand, and said,

"We heard that there is an exhibition here and we came to see it with Ufuk."

"You know you can't go in, right?" said Zeynep.

"Why not, isn't it open to everyone?" Yiğit asked persistently. He was slurring his words when he spoke, with meaningless expressions forming on his face.

EVEN IF IT IS UNREQUITED LOVE, IT MAKES ONE PROUD TO CONFESS IT

46) ALYA CONFESSES HER LOVE TO CEM… 2000

Alya, who went back to Izmir to see Gül and Emin years later, talked to them about her experiences with Cem while they ate fish in Sığacık, where Emin invited her. It was a perfect night when all three of them felt tipsy and the sky was full of shining stars.

They were eating fish and listening to Zeki Müren songs playing there. The conversation got deeper and they talked about funny events from the past, making comments and laughing out loud. As one stopped talking, the other immediately started. They laughed until their stomachs ached at something funny Emin said. While Alya was telling them about something interesting that happened to her at the faculty,

"It was the time when my love for Cem had peaked," she said in passing. Of course, she said that on purpose, and she continued to tell her story as if nothing happened. However, Gül and Emin focused on the word Alya said, they suddenly became serious, and they stopped chewing mid-bite while trying to guess which Cem she was talking about.

They were staring intently at Alya's face now. When they looked at each other to see if the other has heard the same thing, Alya helped them, taking a sip from her drink as if nothing happened, and popping a piece of cheese into her mouth, saying,

"Yes, you heard it right, that Cem you are wondering about is Cem Başar." When she saw them staring at her with shock and questioning eyes, she started from the beginning. She told them about everything from the first meeting in Istanbul, the occasional meetings, the ball they went to, Cem's friend Emre, who courted her, to the meeting on Istiklal Street. For the first time, she shared her feelings in this way, pouring her heart out and crying as she spoke. She also said that the love that started at the faculty did not leave her alone for a long time. Alya brought up this subject because she wanted them to know about those years that she had been keeping a secret, that still made her feel heartache from time to time. Shocked by what they heard, Gül and Emin could not speak, and there was a long silence at the table. Reaching out and putting her hand on Alya's hand, Gül looked at her with tender, questioning eyes.

"You never told me about these things," she said quietly. Emin, who had too much raki and got drunk, was rubbing his beard, his cheeks red and his pupils bright in his blue eyes, thoughtfully looking at the two beautiful women at his table. He believed in his heart that history was repeating itself at the moment, thinking that if something happened once, it could very well happen again. He was the one who broke the silence, saying,

"Alas! Damn it! So my son isn't as lucky as me," and slapping his forehead with his palm. Turning their heads to Emin, the mother and daughter laughed at him. While Gül reached up and wiped Alya's wet cheeks, Emin said,

"I was lucky enough to marry her mother, but he missed

such a cool, smart lady who knows how to drink," trying to cheer them up, but he really felt sorry for his son. Gül was also very sad, but she was also amazed at Alya's reticence on this matter.

Even though it was already over, she was curious about what her daughter had experienced and felt years ago, and she really wanted to know. Before Alya went, she thought that they should definitely talk about this and the details of what happened.

EVERYONE LIVES THEIR OWN DESTINY

47) A PAINFUL EVENT... 2000

Yiğit was at the stage where the first thing he thought about whenever he had money was 'I can buy drugs'. He was on the streets, his social circle was different, he was hopeless and he lived to numb his body. He had truly loved once, and that feeling was not reciprocated. After that, he seemed to be completely detached from life, his behavior and speech showed that he didn't care much about life.

His visits to Füsun had been rare lately as well. When he did visit, he spoke very little and went straight to his room to sleep. He was rarely in the same room with her now, sometimes he could not even tolerate it when Füsun talked, he would immediately snap. The progress of his mother's illness, her weak state, did not seem to affect him much. He didn't feel the slightest pain about Füsun's situation. Füsun knew that these behaviors were directly related to Yiğit, his inner world, and his experiences.

She couldn't do anything about it, she was devastated to see her son like that, to see him disappear before her eyes, and not be able to do anything. She was trying to meet him halfway as much as she could, she spoke to him nicely, but sometimes it was not possible to reach him.

In such an evening again, he yelled over something trivial, and slammed the door, ignoring Füsun's pleas. This was the last night Füsun saw Yiğit.

Two days later, when the phone rang in the middle of the night, Füsun opened her eyes in fear and felt that she was going to hear bad news. She could not get out of bed, she lay on her back with her eyes fixed on the dark ceiling, trying to hear what Zeynep was talking quietly on the phone. Zeynep hung up the phone, but she didn't come to her room. She didn't have the strength to get out of bed and to get the bad news that she was likely to hear from Zeynep. After a while, Zeynep quietly opened her door and looked inside. She knew her mother had woken up to the sound of the phone. Fearing what she might hear, Füsun timidly said,

"Zeynep?". Zeynep sat on the armchair next to her mother's bed, held her hand, and started to gently caress it. Füsun was afraid to ask who had called, so she was waiting silently with her eyes fixed on her daughter's face. Zeynep did not know how to say what she had to say, she remained silent for a few seconds, then slowly said:

"Mom, Yiğit had an accident."

The rest happened behind a curtain of fog for Füsun, and Yiğit was buried a few days later. During this time, Füsun was in shock; she couldn't hear, feel, or speak. For her, everything had lost its importance, her feelings became blunt and words lost their meanings. What was going on around her didn't interest her at all, she just couldn't believe that Yiğit, who was only twenty-four years old, was gone before her. But the thought that her son would be there waiting for her, that she would not be alone, soothed her a bit.

While trying to do a speed test in his friend's car, Yiğit had stepped on the accelerator pedal too hard, and he died along with his friend in the car that flipped over because of high speed. They would never know if it was an accident or suicide.

All of Yiğit's loved ones were present at the cemetery when

he was buried, Füsun saw Gül and her daughters for the first time in years, she accepted condolences when they came to her, and as her tears flowed, she asked God to take her life as soon as possible.

PAIN DECREASES TOLERANCE TOWARDS LIFE

48) ZEYNEP BREAKS UP WITH SINAN… 2000

In fall, the weather in Adana got colder. Zeynep had problems with the people from the municipality for a few days in a row due to a problem with the electric meter installed at her workshop, and apart from that, she also had to deal with some customers and suppliers that drove her crazy. It had been only a few months since Yiğit had died, and the remorse and pain she felt after his death had just begun to subside. Zeynep felt mentally exhausted and had an exhausting week, she told Sinan, who was in the workshop with her on Friday,

"I'm not going to leave home this Saturday, I'm just going to stay in bed all day long." Sinan said that he had a meeting at the newspaper that day, and added,

"You really deserve a rest this week, Zeynep, darling," giving her a kiss on the lips.

Zeynep got up late on Saturday morning and killed time at home. While sipping her afternoon tea and reading Turgut Özakman's new book, "Romantika", the phone rang. She didn't recognize the caller from his voice, who said that she would be grateful to him for what she would see if she went to Sinan's house immediately. Zeynep got angry at the audacity of this person and said,

"If you were a real man, you would also reveal your name and tell me why I should go there."

"I can't tell you that, because it is unspeakably bad," said the unknown person and hung up. Zeynep swore a profanity after him, she was angry that this duffer did not say his name and disturbed her peace while she was trying to read her book. Knowing that there are people who are jealous of their relationship, she did not take the caller seriously at first and continued to read her book. As she turned the pages, it did not take long for her to realize that she did not understand a word from the book because she could not concentrate.

'Why did this anonymous person call out contrary to all reason?', 'What was it that he wanted her to see there?', 'If she didn't go, could she regret it in the future?' Questions she couldn't answer kept swirling around in her head, a sneaky suspicion gnawing at her.

Unable to resist her curiosity any longer, Zeynep decided to go to Sinan's house. She got dressed quickly and left the house and directly went to Sinan's house. Her inner voice told her not to ring the doorbell. She opened the door with her own key and entered the bedroom after hearing the voices.

She froze and couldn't say anything when she looked inside the bedroom through the door. Sinan was in bed

with one of Zeynep's classmates from the faculty, with whom she had an argument before and whom she didn't like at all, in fact, hated, and they were both naked. The sight of them made her sick and she suddenly felt nauseous.

Unable to move, she stood at the door, not knowing what to do. Her head was throbbing, dozens of thoughts were running through her mind. Sinan and Sibel did not know what to do either, they were just looking at Zeynep in shock. Zeynep was the first one to collect herself, and she said,

"You are disgusting!.." turning her back and walking towards the door, ignoring Sinan's pleas. Sinan said,

"Zeynep, listen to me, wait a minute!" and jumped out of the bed, but he could not prevent Zeynep from slamming the door and leaving.

EVERYONE LIVES THEIR OWN LIFE, NOT OTHERS'

49) FÜSUN'S DEATH... 2001

After a long, grueling, and painful period of about four years, Füsun's cancer progressed rapidly, she entered the terminal phase and there was not much left to do. This last period was likely to be shorter and more painful for Füsun.

Füsun's cancer had spread to her liver, and she looked fragile and tiny now. She was breathing hard, her movements slowed down, and she was out of strength to live. The loss of her son had also destroyed her strength to hold on to life. Because of her complaints, she had to be admitted to the hospital very often. Cem and Zeynep, who knew that they might have a few months or days to spend with their mother during this hospitalization and discharge procedures, always wanted to be by her side.

When Cem sent Zeynep home to rest and relax, who was staying with her at the hospital, her mother was constantly and slowly talking about something. Füsun had never been very keen on sharing her memories, but now it looked like she wanted to tell everything all at once.

They turned off the lights and spent a lot of time with her in the quiet hospital room, him on the couch and his mother in bed, in the dim light, where only the bedside lamp was on. Good thing they did. Sometimes Füsun told him what came to her mind as much as her strength allowed. It was during those nights at the hospital when he learned the details of what his mother had gone through with Zeynep and Yiğit when he was not in Adana. And that most things were kept a secret from him so that their problems did not occupy his mind and he could focus on his studies.

Although it was sometimes painful to hear, Cem listened to his mother with interest to learn about her past experiences and feelings; he wanted to stay with his mother all the time as if he wanted to make up for the past years when they couldn't be together much.

It was now very difficult for her to even drink the water due to the narrowing of her esophagus. One day, after bending the straw and drinking only a teaspoon of water with Cem's help, she said,

"You know, sometimes I wish I could remember half of what I've been through and forget the other half," in a barely audible voice.

Pelin, who learned that her mother-in-law's time in the world was limited now, wanted to see her for the sake of the old days. She had not visited or seen her in a long time. She only knew what she was going through as far as Cem told her. There was something she needed to talk to her about, and she had asked her husband to take her with him when he went. One day, when Cem brought Pelin to the hospital, where he was going at every opportunity anyway, they sat together in Füsun's room for a while, silent and sad. Füsun no longer had any strength, she was lying on the bed with her eyes closed. When Cem went downstairs to buy coffee and they were alone, Füsun slowly turned her head towards Pelin.

"I don't have much time left, you know that right?".

"Please don't talk like that, mom," said Pelin. She said that but as she looked at her face, she understood that she knew Cem had problems with Pelin when he spent time at the hospital with her, her son was torn between the two, and he was confused about this.

THE YEARS YOU POSTPONE IN LIFE WILL COME BACK TO YOU AS REGRET IN THE FUTURE

50) ALYA IS AT FÜSUN'S HOUSE… 2001

It had been a week since Füsun had died. At that time, Alya was in Kozan, an hour away from Adana, for a lawsuit. She wanted to see Zeynep, who had just lost her mother, for the sake of old days, what they had given each other and what they learned from each other. Her purpose was to extend her condolences and sit down and have a little chat. She bought her a mosaic cake, which she remembers as her favorite dessert, and since she had also come after Yiğit's death, she found the place easily.

It was not possible for her to inform her because her phone was giving the 'unreachable' signal all the time. Hoping that she was home, she climbed the stairs to the second floor. She knocked on the door and waited. Hearing the sound of the key turning in the lock, she said 'oh thank god she's home', and she was happy and relieved.

A few seconds later, when the door opened, Alya's eyes widened in surprise, seeing someone she never expected.

She stood at the door, not knowing what to say. The person standing in front of her, still very handsome and looking very surprised, was Cem. What Cem saw was a very beautiful woman with a blunt haircut, wavy blonde hair falling to her shoulders, green eyes, a white strapped t-shirt, and a blue denim skirt over her knees, staring at him in surprise. It was Cem who broke the silence, trying to hide his excitement and joy, making a joke and saying,

"Hello, how can I help you? laughing. Alya simply said,

"Hello!" but her heart was beating fast as if it was going to break free out of her rib cage. After a few seconds of staring, as if it just dawned on him, Cem stepped aside and opened the door to let her in,

"Come in," he said. Alya walked into the living room, standing in the middle of the room, and said, "I guess Zeynep is not at home," as she put the cake box she had brought on the coffee table.

He said, "She had some work that she had to do, so she went to the workshop."

"I heard that Mrs. Füsun had been in the hospital for a long time. She must have had very hard days," Alya said in a sad voice.

"Yes, she was in the hospital and she really suffered a lot towards the end," said Cem, taking a deep breath.

THE VALUE OF THINGS LIKE LIFE IS APPRECIATED TOO LATE

51) EMİN'S TOLERANCE FOR LIFE DECREASES... 2005

Just like when Gül questioned the past and her own attitude when she found out Dila decided to wear hijab, Emin started to question himself after Yiğit's death.

Everything started after Emin, who was sixty years old when Yiğit died, buried him and returned to Urla from Adana. Although it was a beautiful spring season, when nature was starting to come to life, Emin's perceptions were dark, like his soul. In those times when he was thinking about the past over and over, the thought that he neglected his children by prioritizing his own pleasures felt like a knife in his heart, being turned over from time to time. He had come to rely on alcohol to relieve the pain of the wound this knife had inflicted on his conscience.

It was as if his mind was haunted by terrible memories, and particularly one of them was popping up and suffocating him. He would always remember the day he took Yiğit to treatment about eight years ago. He couldn't forget Yiğit's accusing attitude and his disregard for him. And that it was one of the worst days of his life... Füsun also died a year after Yiğit's death. He was just beginning to understand that life went by fast as children grew up and that as they got older, there was not as much time left for other things desired to do.

Things were not going well at the hospital where Emin worked at that time, either, and it was now more difficult to deal with bureaucracy and to meet the demands imposed on him. Even the routine tasks that didn't even bother him before were making him exhausted. His tolerance for life had declined by a lot. He had nothing to worry about but being calm and peaceful; all he wanted was to run towards happiness.

In the evenings, he was usually nervous, taking his drink as soon as he came home and sitting in front of the TV. He couldn't relax without drinking a few glasses every night, he couldn't calm the restlessness inside him. His relationship with his friends had also diminished; the old cheerful talkative Emin was gone, replaced by an angry, unhappy Emin who did not hesitate to hurt people.

He also misunderstood many things Gül said, warned him about, or shared with good intentions, and he was looking for an ulterior motive in any word and in any event. At that time, Gül made a great effort to help him, but Emin resisted her and never agreed to cooperate. Maintaining a marriage with Emin, who was constantly in an aggressive mood and who was developing an intolerable character, now required extreme effort from Gül. Gül felt that the distance between them was gradually getting longer, their relationship was slowly slipping out of her hands, and it was painful for her to be unable to retain it and to watch helplessly as it happened. According to her, one could not spend the whole life regretting something.

As the years passed by, Emin began to withdraw more and more. It was as if he had built a wall around himself, imprisoned himself within that wall, and isolated himself from the outside world. The only thing he knew was that the times when he thought about Adana were the shining hours of his boring and monotonous days. He wouldn't let anyone in to reach him. Now he always lived in the past, seizing every opportunity to tell Gül about the times he spent with his children and got angry if she didn't want to listen. He often told the same things over and over; while listening to these, Gül was becoming exasperated. There was hardly a day when they didn't argue. One evening, while Emin was sitting on the veranda drinking his wine, Gül had come from outside. When Emin said,

"I want to talk to you", Gül felt that it was something serious, and grumbled,

"I hope it's good." She climbed up several steps of the stairs separating the veranda from the garden and said,

"I'll change and be right back," and went inside. When Gül came back, he started speaking,

"I want to die in the lands where I was born, where I spent a portion of my life, where I lost my son and my children's mother," and continued:

"At this age, I want to work with soil, I want to walk barefoot on soil rather than sand from now on, I want to breathe in the smell of soil soaked in rain," he said.

"I have a different kind of pain in my heart, close to real pain, but feels like being breathless or suffocating," he said.

Emin's speech was thought thoroughly and intellectualized, and the final decision was taken. Gül had listened to him silently as he said many things like these. After her husband's speech was over,

"I respect your decision, I hope you will be alone in your action like this decision you took by yourself," she said. But Emin could not fully understand Gül's last sentence, even though he knew she loved the sea and Urla and she wouldn't come with him, he joked,

IF LOVE IS REAL, IT CONTINUES FROM WHERE IT WAS LEFT OFF DESPITE EVERYTHING

52) EACH LIFE IS A NOVEL... 2010

Zeynep, who had opened and ventilated the workshop and was sipping her morning coffee, turned her gaze in that direction with the sound of the doorbell and saw Aycan hurriedly entering.

"What happened, did you see me in your dream last night?" she said, smiling. Aycan was a friend from university, and she had been seeing her for years. She was one of the rare people with whom she shared everything about her life.

Aycan said "Good morning," threw herself on the couch, and directly began the conversation.

"Dear Zeynep, there's a new book on the market, it's very popular, have you heard of it?".

"Good morning to you too," said Zeynep. She was sipping her coffee while staring at Aycan, thinking 'I wonder what she is going on about this time'.

"Did you come in the early morning to recommend a book

to me?" said Zeynep with questioning eyes.

"Yes, exactly like that," said Aycan.

"So you liked it that much?" Zeynep asked.

"Yeah, I like it, but the thing is…" she paused.

"What's the name of the book?"

"Each Life Is A Novel,"

"No, I haven't read it," said Zeynep.

"Zeynep, I read this book and finished it late at last night. I could hardly wait for the morning to come here," she said.

"To recommend it to me?" Zeynep asked, looking in disbelief.

"Zeynep, you may not believe it, but this book is about you," said Aycan.

"What do you mean about me?" she raised her eyebrows, looking at Aycan as if trying to understand.

"You, I mean, you and your family. Yiğit, Cem, and even your step-sisters…"

"There may be many novels similar to our lives"

"There can't be that many similarities. Your illness, Yiğit's addiction, the elder brother who is a doctor, lawyer sister, sister who wears hijab…"

"God, all these are in the book?"

"Besides, the characters live in Adana, and the father and his wife live in Urla."

"So you're saying it can't be a coincidence"

"Absolutely not, Zeynep," said Aycan. She said that she wanted to bring the book but her curious mother took it when she told her about it before leaving home. Zeynep, who made Aycan repeat the name and author of the book,

left the workshop saying, "Don't go anywhere until I return, wait here." She bought the book in question from the bookstore, which was ten minutes' walk away, and came back. It was a 240-page book with an illustration of a large tree on the cover, and she had never heard of the author before.

Aycan left the workshop saying "I'll leave you alone so you can start reading, let's meet again when you're finished". Zeynep could never have guessed that her whole life would change in ways she could never have foreseen after reading this book at that time.

She read the book, which was not very thick, whenever she had the opportunity. Except for when she had to take a break from it -the students she taught, the meeting with the manager of a company she worked with, a visiting friend- she continued to read both at the workshop and at home.

She couldn't put it down while eating and even on the toilet. Some chapters she had to go back and read over and over again. When she finished the book, she heard the sound of the morning prayer coming from the mosque and Zeynep was in awe. It was really about herself, her family, what they went through, and the most private moments in their lives. The book ended after Füsun's death. Some events were probably fictionalized because the author's knowledge about their life was insufficient and those parts did not correspond to reality. But there was also information that was surprisingly impossible for anyone to know.

She had never heard of the author before, it was possible that someone familiar with her life had told things to the author. Who could that be? Could Yiğit have told him before he died? But there was no way he knew that much detail, and he wouldn't have bothered with such a thing. Gül, Alya or Dila were among the first to come to mind. But why would they tell? Could it be for money? She didn't think so, they wouldn't do such a thing. She was very confused. She searched the Internet for information about the author; she found nothing but the fact that it was his first book. It was as if the author had done everything to be unreachable.

In the meantime, Zeynep went to her father to ask if he knew something, she left the book with him, and asked him to read it. Emin, who was seventy years old and lived in Adana at the time, did not take Zeynep's stories seriously and thought, 'It's just Zeynep's paranoia.'

"Okay, I'll read it, leave it there," he said carelessly. But when he called her on the phone a few days later, he too was in awe.

"I told Gül about the book, too, and she couldn't believe it. She might call you so you know," said Emin.

After a lot of effort, Zeynep learned by chance that the author of the book used a pseudonym; in fact, there was no one by that name. After learning this, the first person that came to her mind was Sinan, her ex-boyfriend with whom she had been together for many years. After catching him in bed with someone else about ten years ago, they had never seen each other again. It was a period when Zeynep didn't care about the world, when she really wanted to vanish. It was very difficult for her to go through this period, she was only able to survive with her medication, she was made to sleep all the time.

EVERYONE PLAYS THEIR OWN PART IN LIFE

53) PELIN TELLS CEM SHE WANTS A DIVORCE... 2012

They had to move to Adana and settle there after getting married since Cem was accepted to the residency training there, but Pelin could never adapt to there and was unhappy.

A successful orthopedist, Cem was a very busy physician. Ever since he came to Adana, he received a lot of support from his own family and friends, he was getting increasingly popular and the number of his patients was increasing day by day. He was good at his job, and he was happy with the compliments he received. His priorities in life were his son and his job.

He always encouraged Pelin about the things she could do. From the very beginning of their marriage, as she said that she was bored in Adana, he repeated at every opportunity that he was ready to financially and morally support her to start a business and become her own boss. In the beginning, Pelin leaned towards this idea; she even did research on a few things to start a business for a long time. Later on, she lost her enthusiasm and gave up on it. Cem saw that Pelin did not know what she wanted, it was difficult for him to understand her, but he definitely thought that she was someone who did not know how to be happy.

Pelin's unhappiness also affected their relationship. When Cem was not on duty and he was at home, they always had an argument about something. Sometimes their arguments got so big that it took a lot of effort to get their relationship back on track. Therefore, Cem mostly preferred to work shifts at the hospital.

Another characteristic of Pelin was that she would leave home after their arguments and was not seen for a few days until her anger subsided. At such times, she was going to her aunt living in Ceyhan, to a friend, or to a hotel. After a particularly bad argument they had, she even left Adana and went to her family in Istanbul. She went away, but because her relationship with her sister and mother was not very good either, she could not stay with them long, and she returned saying that she had missed her son. At that time, Tuna was going to primary school. She admitted that what she did was a mistake and apologized to Cem.

In another big argument, Tuna was going to secondary school at the time, and this time she stayed with a friend in Bursa. It wasn't easy for Cem to convince Pelin to return home, he had to make a lot of effort. He went to Bursa, and his effort to bring Pelin back to Adana cost him a high-carat diamond ring.

After the arguments, Cem told her many times that he didn't like it when Pelin left their son and him like that. "It is very important for me that my son grows up with his mother and father," he emphasized all the time. In a determined tone, he would say,

"We both have to make an effort to keep and maintain our relationship for Tuna," and he really put a lot of effort into it. Pelin was an unconcerned mother, she was not as sensitive as Cem about Tuna.

"Your child can be happy only if you are happy," she would say to Cem.

She would also say, "There is no need to pretend we are happy for Tuna, we are what we are" and keep going her own way. Despite Pelin, Cem always made sacrifices for their child throughout their marriage. He was doing his best so that he grew up with both his parents.

Cem thought Tuna was a lot like his late uncle; both his personality and his physical characteristics were the same. In Tuna's reactions to some events, he felt like he saw Yiğit in front of him. When people around them talked about this similarity, they would always add,

"Let his fate be different." Tuna was his sensitive spot, even though he knew that his fate was not going to be similar, that it was impossible. Still, he felt a slight fear about it from time to time. If Pelin had to leave Adana permanently, she would take her son with her to Istanbul; the thought of Tuna growing up apart from him terrified Cem.

Years passed, and Tuna was in his last year of high school. He was preparing for the university entrance exam with all his might, by going to school during the daytime, to the study center in the evening, and to the private classes on the weekends. As always, Cem was paying the utmost attention not to negatively affect his child who needed to study, and he was careful to not let his arguments with Pelin get worse so that their son was not affected by them. Therefore, the miscommunication at home continued in the form of the cold war; they were both living in their own world. Tuna, who devoted himself to his lessons, was almost only at home to sleep.

It was the last days of July when Tuna was sent to summer camp to rest after he took the university entrance exam. Those were the times when the hot summer days of Adana made people tired and unable to move. As every summer, the patient visits decreased, and the work at the hospital was lighter.

For the safety of their nuclear family, Cem decided to surprise Pelin, who was very tired because of the sacrifices they made for their son as he was studying so that she would get away from home a little bit and boost her morale. Moreover, Pelin's birthday coincided with the date they would be there. They would spend time alone and have the opportunity to work on their relationship. Thinking this way, Cem booked a luxury hotel in Antalya Belek. But, as it turned out, Pelin didn't like a fait accompli that was put in front of her in this way. Pelin had looked forward to the end of Tuna's university entrance exam, and she was not feeling well at that time. No one knew that she had other plans and was confused about how to implement those plans.

When Cem made his offer with great joy, she said,

"I'm not in the mood for a vacation at all right now, sorry." At first, Cem tried to convince her, but when he saw she was determined, he gave up.

"I'll call tomorrow and cancel the reservation then," he said and went to bed angrily. While he was wearing his pajamas, he thought again that Pelin 'doesn't know what she wants and doesn't want to be happy' and was angry with himself for having good intentions. The next morning, before Cem left the house, Pelin said,

"Don't cancel the reservation, I thought during the night and decided to go to Antalya," said Pelin. While ensuring Tuna's comfort at home – she took great care of her son's diet, took him to private classes, most of the time by car- and made a lot of effort to keep his motivation high, she was also really tired as well. It would also be good for her to get away from this place and go out of the city. Besides, maybe she could put into effect the plan that was running in her head, waiting for the right time to realize it.

Four days later, they set out in the early morning by car. Their journey had been quiet, and they didn't talk much in the car. They listened to a lot of music, stopped to drink tea when they saw a beautiful place. When they arrived in Belek and settled in the hotel, they both felt satisfied. A warm weather greeted them in Belek as well. Despite everything, people were doing their best to make the most of their vacation and enjoy the hotel.

After going downstairs and having their breakfast quietly in the morning, they went to their rooms and put on their swimsuits, and then decided what they wanted to do that day. Cem was reading on the beach, going to the gym, swimming, and jogging on the beach. Pelin, on the other hand, preferred the pool and sauna, had a massage, or preferred to relax in the hotel room. It was a quiet and peaceful vacation. They would usually come together for dinner, check the activities offered by the hotel after dinner, and then retreat to their room.

On the evening of the third day of their stay at the hotel, after they had dinner, they watched an animation show and went back to their room. However, the moon was extra beautiful that night. The starry sky and a gentle breeze blowing for the first time since they had arrived were tempting. Neither of them had any desire to enjoy that beautiful night. As they both got very tired during the day, all they wanted now was to get in bed and sleep.

While Pelin was in the bathroom to remove her make-up, Cem was on the phone with a friend from Adana who asked his opinion about a patient's surgery. Pelin thought in the bathroom and made a decision, after a while, she came out and put her arms together, standing in the middle of the room. She stared thoughtfully at Cem, frowned, waiting for Cem's phone call to end. Realizing that Pelin was going to say something to him, Cem finished speaking, approached Pelin, and tried to hold her hand. While trying to free her hands from him, she uttered the sentence that shocked Cem,

"Cem, I want a divorce," she said. Cem stood still, stunned, unable to say anything.

"I can't take it anymore, there's no point in continuing like this. I was waiting for Tuna to take the university entrance exam to tell you this," she added. He could not say anything. He was staring at Pelin silently. Lastly, Pelin uttered the magic sentence that meant a lot to Cem:

"Besides, if you want, Tuna can stay with you," she said. Cem still didn't know what to say, he just looked at Pelin thoughtfully.

"I didn't want to say it in a place like this, I'm sorry I ruined your vacation..." While Cem was walking towards the door of the room, he raised his hand to prevent Pelin from saying anything more,

"I'll get some fresh air," he said, slammed the door behind himself, and left the room.

He started walking towards the most deserted, remotest point of the holiday village, where the sports facilities were located. He felt nothing, neither anger nor sadness. He just walked, saw, and felt: the silence of the hotel, the bungalows lined up on green lawns, the scent of jasmines by the road, the rustle of palm leaves in the wind, and the overwhelming urge to smoke.

A little further on, he saw a young man who was removing covers from tables as the place was closed and people wouldn't come after that hour, and he asked him,

"Hey man, do you smoke?".

"Unfortunately I don't," said the boy.

"Give this abandoned man a drink and please find a cigarette," he said as he sat down at a table with its cover still on. Smoking a cigarette would calm him down. The boy ran off and soon returned with a single cigarette in one hand and a glass of vodka in the other. The boy who received a big tip from Cem for this was very happy and said,

"Thanks, sir," looking at the money in his hand. To the young boy who looked seventeen or eighteen, he said,

"Sit down!" pointing to the chair opposite him. Looking at Cem's face with curiosity and trying to understand what happened, the boy timidly sat on the chair.

Cem started to talk, he told the boy sitting in front of him about his whole life, while the boy refreshed his drink a few more times. Towards the end of his story, which he began to tell from his childhood, he was no longer trying to stop his tears.

While the boy handed him the napkins on the table, he was looking at Cem with interest, shaking his head from time to time, making a comment or two occasionally. Perhaps for the first time in his life, he confessed to someone he did not know that he did not love Pelin as much as he loved Alya. He told, told, and told without knowing how many hours he had been sitting there and talking... After many hours, he said,

"I have to go now," struggling to get up from the table and regain his balance. With difficulty standing and slurring his words, he said,

"You are such a good listener, my friend!" putting his hand in his pocket and giving all the money in his pocket to the boy. The boy, who received almost half of his monthly salary, could not believe his eyes.

Leaving there after saying "Take care," Cem felt light as a feather as he was walking towards his room, swaying with a smile on his face...

THE PLACE WHERE YOU DEFINE YOURSELF IS IMPORTANT

54) AFTERWORD...

Dila, who was pregnant when Yiğit died, gave birth shortly after his death and named the baby 'Yiğit'. (2000) Cem and Pelin divorced in a short time. (2012) After the divorce, Cem moved in with Emin, who had been living in Adana since 2005. Tuna, who got into Çukurova University Faculty of Medicine, lived in the same house with his grandfather and father for a while. Three men, three generations, who had different perspectives on life, had a great time during their stay together. The lessons on respecting women and their values were given instantly to Tuna by the other two when needed. He was learning things about women, learning from his father's and grandfather's experiences, had a lot of fun listening to their interesting memories; he entertained them in return as well. Tuna was a cheerful and humorist boy who focused on the good things in life. He would do both Emin and Cem a power of good.

After Cem got divorced and put his life in order with his son, the subject of talking to Alya, which was always in his mind, made him very uneasy. He wanted her so badly and would call her eventually, but the prospect of being rejected by Alya was terrifying, and he got discouraged every time he thought about it.

Emin, who was now seventy-two years old and had to take medication regularly due to newly emerging diseases, spoke slowly one evening when they were sitting together, and said,

"You know what, Cem? There are three phases in life: youth phase, middle-age phase, and 'you look good' phase," he said, shaking his head. To his son, who was now forty-four, he said with a smile,

"Life is passing by, you mustn't miss that wonderful girl. It would be a shame for you both if you missed your chance again," he said.

After a few days, Cem plucked up all his courage and called Alya excitedly.

"Alya, we need to talk right now," he said, taking a plane the next day, going straight to her. When they got together, he knelt before her and asked her to marry him.

He had to say many things such as "I'll do whatever you want, just say it", and he finally convinced her. At the dinner they came together to celebrate this, Cem said,

"You know what I noticed, Alya?" and as Alya looked at him with questioning eyes, he said,

"While it is actually possible to solve problems at the root, the energy that a person spends to solve them and the compromises that have to be made in life is the real thing that makes life complicated for a person," Alya said,

"So you just realized this?" smiling sarcastically, and he replied,

"Another thing that complicates life is the amount and intensity of the compromises you have to make in your life," he said.

"It's a really heavy burden to carry," Alya said in response.

Alya, who fell madly in love with Cem after getting to know him, couldn't be with anyone after realizing that no one could replace him. Until that moment, she had buried her love in her heart and continued working as a successful lawyer. Years later, while telling her story to Tuna's daughter, she would say 'I always had the hope that I would be with Cem eventually and it never diminished'.

About a year and a half after the divorce, Cem and Alya got married (2014) and settled in Adana. The three handsome men, after sharing the same house for months and having a great time, were no longer flatmates. This time Alya, Cem and Tuna became a family. Alya and Tuna got along very well and loved each other very much.

Zeynep married Sinan and settled in Istanbul. Much later, Sinan's book would be made into a movie that Zeynep would watch with sadness. When the idea came from a producer to make the book into a movie, they put a lot of thought into it. Later, Zeynep said about the movie,

"It was a painful experience for me to see it." Because nothing in the movie was true. Seeing the two families' mutual attitudes, yes, she felt something familiar for a moment, but the movie was not about the children of the two families. The film was about how the mother of one family and the father of another family looked at each other and fell in love. The mother in the movie was struggling with the weight of her infidelity, running her hand through her long blonde hair—Gül never had long blonde hair—and crying. The mother in the movie was under pressure from all sides: the health center where she worked, her children, her lover, his children, her friends. Her poor husband didn't seem to want anything from her, he was picking up the plates in the kitchen. In the film, the children of both families were also ignored, as if they were not found worthy of attention. Dilek Ozsoyler-2021-Adana